Flights of the Mind

Lorraine James

Some of the stories in this collection have been previously
published in the following:
Fellowship of Australian Writers (FAW) *Writers' Voice*
Southern Highlands FAW Anthologies Potpourri 2021 &
Tilting at Windmills 2024
Life's Toolbox Trilogy
Seniors' Stories Vol 7 & 9

First published 2026 by
Ginninderra Press
PO Box 2 Bentleigh 3204
ginninderrapress.com.au

Contents

CORONATION ROAD
1921 - UPHEAVAL

They were standing in Martin Place.

Mum called out –

'But what about the children...?'

'They can go to hell!'

Dad was shouting. His usually composed and rather bland face was bright red. Furious, he turned and strode away, disappearing around the corner of the General Post Office.

Mummy stood very still. Bid was holding onto her gloved hand. She was holding on very tight. Her brother Tom was standing close by but not touching. At ten years' old it was as if he was trying to appear independent and grown up. What was going on? Was he now the man of the family? He dropped his head, looking down, embarrassed, hands in his pockets, scuffling his boots on the pavement. He stood on one foot and scuffed his boot around in a circle. Then he did the other one.

It seemed that crowds of people were walking all around them, this way and that. Brushing past. Some scowled, looking irritated as if the clustered group of three were in their way. Bid felt like they were on a little round island, inanimate actors in a movie when the projector breaks down and the scene on the screen is frozen. The space around them seemed to be their space exclusively and the whirling crowds outside their orbit caused them to feel confused and consumed and drawn right inside its frightening vortex.

Eventually, as if emerging from a trance, Mummy squeezed Bid's hand and laying her arm around Tom's shoulder she said, 'Come along. We'll get the tram now.'

The safety zone was crowded. The tram was crowded but a gentleman, courteously lifting his hat, stood up and gave his seat to Mrs. Briggs. Bid and Tom stood close beside her – leaning against her – wanting to maintain physical contact. And anyway, they weren't tall enough yet to reach the swinging leather straps and had to hold onto the end of the seat backs to steady themselves as the tram, when it got up speed between stops, was racketing along, rocking and swaying at times.

Eventually they disembarked at their stop and walked quickly towards home. They turned into their street, passing the house on the corner that had a letter box that looked, in miniature, exactly like the house it belonged to. Usually they'd comment on it, it was so quaint and delightful. But today nothing had been said by anyone since Mummy had said 'Come along...'

Inside the house she went straight into her bedroom where Bid and Tom knew, standing outside the door, that she would be taking off her hat and coat and changing her shoes. Very soon she appeared and headed up the long hallway towards the back of the house. She went into the breakfast room and into the tiny kitchenette beyond and started taking food out of the safe in the pantry. The safe had four legs which stood in four bowls of water to foil ants.

Bid and Tom followed her, standing beside the table in the breakfast room and when she emerged, tying her apron at the back, she said sharply, 'Well, don't stand about. Go and change your clothes and put on something warm. Then you can go out to the woodshed and fill up the coal scuttle.'

She knelt down in front of the fireplace, pulling kindling out of one of the storage stools on either side of the hearth and building a neat little construction in the grate, topped by a couple of bark-covered logs of wood.

Tom and Bid ran out the backdoor and down the verandah steps. The woodshed was enveloped by a brilliant scarlet bougainvillea. One day Bid was sure she had seen a fairy in the tangly creeper. There it was, high up amongst the blooms, all pink and fluffy. It flew off, the sun shining through its wings and Tom said 'It's a'naphid, silly.' But Bid was sure it was a fairy. She did a quick check before they entered the coal shed which smelt all lovely and woody because of the big pile of firewood that Dad had chopped only yesterday... before he left.

But had he left? What did he mean?

Tom was thinking, 'Why do we have to light a fire when it isn't really very cold?' But then he thought of his mother when she emerged from her bedroom. She had a cardigan on and she was wrapping it around the front of her and, as she walked up the hall ahead of them, her arms folded, she seemed all sort of bent over. He felt worried about her. He had an awful feeling of foreboding and muttered, 'Something really bad's going on here.'

They brought the scuttle in and Tom was allowed to toss a few lumps of coal into the flames.

Mum said, 'What do you fancy for dinner?' and both chorused 'Crumpets!'

Their mother didn't say no so they raced to the drawer in the dresser and got out the toasting forks and then they sat on either side of the fireplace on the storage stools. Impaling a crumpet on each fork they leant forward to toast them over the flames. Tiny sparks marched around in the soot at the back of the fireplace. 'Soldiers' they called them. Then Mummy brought in three plates with three knives and a block of butter and three mugs of lovely hot cocoa and moving a dining chair forward, sat down between them, leaning towards the fire with a crumpet on her fork. After a while Bid and Tom said 'Swap?' and they exchanged places because the side of their bodies nearest the fire were toasting, like the crumpets.

'This is rather like Sunday nights.' Bid ventured, tentatively giving her mother a smile. Madeleine Briggs glanced at her briefly, nodded and looked back into the fire. Bid wondered whether she'd glimpsed a sad little smile, a grateful response? But she wasn't sure. The three of them sat in silence staring into the flames.

***

Next morning Mum spent a lot of time on the telephone talking with Grandad and Tom and Bid spent just as much time hovering out of sight in various rooms nearby – trying to glean some meaning from the conversations. If she spotted them Mummy kept shooing them away and telling them to 'Go out and play'. They mucked around outside for a while but couldn't settle to anything. Tom kept muttering, 'Something's up' over and over again until Bid told him to shut up. Her tummy was all tight and sore and she felt frightened.

She felt she might be sick.

Then they heard footsteps on the gravel and here came Grandad striding around from the side of the house, moustached, wearing his grey suit with its fob chain and his homburg on his head. He gave them both an affectionate tickle on their cheeks and without speaking, strode up the back steps and inside.

Bid sat down on the verandah steps and thought about the other night when she had woken up because she heard Mummy crying out. It was coming from the breakfast room at the back of the house, not from the big bedroom at the front that her parents shared.

She crept out in her bare feet, avoiding the floorboards where she knew they cracked. The door was slightly ajar so she peeked. Dad was twisting Mummy's arm right up her back and saying something in her ear. He was speaking very quietly and Mum was trying not to make a noise even though Bid knew she was in pain. Then Dad let go and pushing Mummy hard against the table, he turned towards the door. Bid shot down the hall and hid behind one of the heavy velvet curtains that were tied back halfway down beside the telephone table and, because the hall was in darkness, without spying her, Dad walked past her and along into the big bedroom.

Tippy toeing back into her room, wishing so much she was brave enough to check on her mother, Bid climbed back into bed and lay like a statue. Her whole body was tense as, after what seemed ages, she heard the light switch in the breakfast room snap off and her mother's steps start along the hallway. They stopped outside Bid's room. The door quietly opened. Bid closed her eyes tight. Mummy came in and stood close to her bed. Bid could hear her taking little sobby breaths. A kiss, as light as a butterfly, touched her cheek. Bid listened as Tom's door opened. A moment's silence, then she heard her mother come quietly out into the hall again and the faint brushy sound of her slippers on the carpet runner fade away.

Bid and Tom knew Dad drank. Anyone could see that. It wasn't every night that he'd come home inebriated (Tom had picked up that new word from the crime reports in the newspaper). When Dad hadn't been drinking he was a nice gentlemanly sort of Cove (this moniker provided by Tom's best mate Ted who made a hobby of collecting terms from the World War 1 vernacular). Yes, he was generally an okay Dad but when he'd been drinking it was quite a different story. He'd shout at Mum and swear and be extremely obnoxious and sometimes slap her. And Mum, who was a real lady, would get frightened and upset although, despite her reserved manner, she did show some spunk now and then. Her sister Aunty Florence, known as Flo, used to say things about Mum like 'It's the Irish in her' or 'Maddy's no walkover'.

Dad seldom did these things to Tom and Bid because generally, when he came home drunk, they were already in bed. But they often stayed awake until he came home – not on purpose – but because they couldn't get to sleep until they found out what sort of mood he was in.

***

The children were still hanging around in the garden – 'wasting time' according to Tom who was complaining about being bored when suddenly Mum appeared at the back door and called out, 'Come inside both of you.'

She didn't even say 'please' which was unusual so Bid and Tom leapt the steps two at a time and shot into the house. They weren't in the breakfast room – Mum and Grandad – they were in the sitting room.

'Serious' Tom thought as he and Bid slowed down and entered the room.

Mum gave them a wobbly sort of smile and in a trembly voice said, 'Grandad would like you to come and stay with him for a few days. We'll pack the Pullman bags for you – that's all you'll need in the meantime.'

Tom was quick to pick up on the phrase 'in the meantime'. That was interesting but he said, 'What about school? Will we be able to go or is it a holiday? Y'know – if it's just for a few days?'

'Oh you'll go to school. It's much the same distance from Grandad's as it is from here. You can walk as usual. Now come along – we'll go and sort out some clothes.'

'Are we going now? Right away?' Bid was feeling really sick now. She loved Grandad and she loved his house but this was all very worrying.

Mummy said reassuringly, 'Yes – why not? No point in waiting' and she headed out the door.

***

They were in Grandad's car. It was huge and shiny and black. It had polished brown ribbed leather seats and Bid, who had been relegated the back seat because she was the smallest and, she suspected, a girl, was having trouble sitting still because every time they went around a corner she'd slide from one side to the other.

Grandad was to blame. He was a terrible driver. All the family talked about it. They said he thought he "owned the road". When they got to an intersection he wouldn't even stop. He wouldn't even slow down. He'd just put his hand on the horn and roar through! It was terrifying, especially that day there were two trams coming towards each other from both directions and he just shot across the tram lines between them. That episode was a family legend. Bid couldn't wait until they reached Coronation Road and, into the bargain, she had this overwhelming desire to bop Tom on the head with something because he was sitting up in front as if he owned the entire world and pretending to look unconcerned about Grandad's driving. She was starting to look around in her Pullman for a weapon – 'Ah a book! Perfect!' when Grandad said, 'Well – here we are' and Bid suddenly shot across and slammed into the right hand corner of the back seat as he made a violent left turn into the driveway and sped along beside the house and around into the back yard.

People came tumbling out the kitchen door.

'Louise! Thomas! Hello! How lovely to see you.' They were enveloped in Aunty Flo's generous embrace and had their faces squeezed into her pillowy chest. What was she doing here? She didn't live here. But that was immediately forgotten when Uncle John came limping towards them, a smile on his gentle face, his right hand folded down against his waist. He was shy so he didn't embrace them and anyway he couldn't really, having only one arm that worked. Mum had told them he'd been 'Damaged at Birth' and that was what made him so amiable.

Then Aunt Mildred stepped forward. Her welcome wasn't nearly as warm but she gave them both a tight smile and a pat on the shoulder and said, 'Come inside both of you. Afternoon tea's ready.'

***

No. 8 Coronation Road was a big house. It was a sprawling white painted villa with verandahs decorated with filigree trims and two wings at right angles with generous bay windows. Inside a wide central hall ran from front to back with rooms issuing out on either side. There were six bedrooms although one of the largest ones at the front of the house was currently used as a billiard room.

The house sat on acreage with an orchard, fowls, ducks and a large aviary. Across the back yard there was a long building containing a stable for the horse and trap, a garage for the Wolesley and a tool shed that also stored the firewood, coal and general flotsam and jetsam. There was also a laundry known as "the wash house". On the Northern side of the house there was a lawn tennis court.

Bid and Tom loved visiting Grandad's place but they had never slept there before. Aunt Mildred took them along the hall and showed them their rooms which were beside each other. She told them to unpack their bags and which drawers to put their meagre assortment of clothes in and told them to hang their school uniforms in their wardrobes.

'After you've done that' she said, 'come into the drawing room and have some afternoon tea.'

Walking back along the hall Tom nudged Bid and whispered 'Brown buns, yum.' And Bid smiled and nodded.

The tea trolley was already in place and the desired buns were on the bottom shelf. Aunty Flo presided, pouring everyone cups of tea which obviously irritated Aunt Mildred who sat and scowled. After all, she lived here – Florence didn't. Grandad was sitting in his wing chair at the bay window, reading. He had cataracts so he had his glasses on and a magnifying glass. Uncle John had a little side table at his left elbow with his cup of tea on it because that was the only arm he could use.

The afternoon meandered on in the same pattern as it always did when they were making their regular Sunday visits. The only thing that was different was that Mummy and Dad weren't there.

****

Bid woke next morning in her unfamiliar room. She hopped out of bed, put on her dressing gown and padded up to the bathroom which straddled the end of the hall. It had a door with a vibrant window made of a variety of coloured squares of stained glass which were all sort of bobbly so you couldn't see the person inside. The linoleum was cold on Bid's bare feet.

She came out and turned left into the kitchen. It was a vast room with copper pots and pans hanging in rows and a clothesline with a pulley stretched high up in front of the black wood stove. There was a long scrubbed wooden table under which were hung, in muslin bundles, this season's puddings, waiting for Christmas. These would have been thoroughly soaked in brandy before they were hung to ripen.

Eileen, the live-in household helper, privately known by the family as 'But It's M'night Orf', was standing at the enormous porcelain sink, rinsing dishes.

'ullo Young Lady.' she said, beaming at Bid. Then before Bid could enter into an interesting conversation with Eileen (she had a fund of stories generally with a grizzly or tragic bent), Aunt Mildred appeared and said, 'Louise! Why are you in your bare feet? Go and put your school uniform on at once and then come and have your porridge. *And* go and wake up that lazy brother of yours.'

***

Grandad drove them to school that morning. He wanted to be sure they knew the way from Coronation Road. He said, 'Now, you'll be walking home so be observant while we are driving there so you remember the way back.'

'He said 'Home' Tom remarked to Bid as they entered the school gates. 'Something's up.'

'Oh shut up.' Bid headed off in the direction of her classroom. She knew Tom was right of course but he was such a know-it-all. Something very disturbing was indeed 'Up'.

***

During their first few days at Grandad's, Mum kept in touch by phone but there was no communication from Dad. Then, a day or two later, when the children arrived home from school they were amazed to see a removal truck parked at the front door and two men unloading furniture that belonged in their house in Ashton Road. They were carrying everything into the billiard room including their mother's treadle sewing machine.

The billiard table was gone. There were two single beds placed at right angles in the corner at one end of the room and a small round dining table with three chairs in the middle. A chesterfield and two comfy armchairs had been arranged in the bay window at the other end.

They raced back out the front door chorusing

'What's going on? What's happening?'

Their mother said

'We're going to be staying here for a while but let me explain everything once we've finished unloading.' She walked up to them and put her arms around both of them at once, gave them a huge hug and then turned back. Her face had that twisty look when a person is trying not to cry so Bid and Tom headed down the hallway to the kitchen to see if Eileen had baked something yummy for an after-school snack.

ACTION

Madeleine Briggs climbed the stairs to the first floor of the legal office located in the city's main street. She was visiting the senior partner, Sir Richard Carpenter KC. He had been handling her father, John Garwick Walsh's legal affairs since the 1880s and now, in 1921, she hoped they were going to assist her in settling her own.

The day after the children had driven off with Father to Coronation Road she made an immediate appointment to see Sir Richard. She wanted to get his advice about how to legally handle the matter of a separation from her husband Mathew Briggs. She was determined to achieve a complete estrangement but she also had certain conditions that she hoped she could fulfil. Sir Richard greeted her most courteously. He had already been briefed about Mrs Briggs' circumstances by her father and was interested to meet the eldest daughter of his old client and friend.

As he stood to greet her he saw a slight, elegant young woman – in her thirties he would guess and very softly spoken. She had a fragility about her but, having shaken his hand and sat down firmly on her chair, she instigated their discussions immediately.

'Thank you for seeing me so promptly' she began. 'I realise this is no longer a part of your legal brief but I know, as a friend, my father has already spoken to you and so you know I am here to obtain your assistance and advice about the matter of separating from my husband. Do you think it would be best for me to first of all tell you what I want?'

Sir Richard nodded.

'It's simple. I want him to sign over our house solely to me.' She settled back in her chair, adjusting her handbag on her lap, smoothing and patting it repeatedly, betraying her underlying anxiety.

'Well... that's a tall order. Do you realise, in the matter of divorce, how the law lies?'

'I do. But all I want is the house.'

The KC was astonished. This was a perfect example of the metaphor "Never judge a book by its cover". He was a bit flummoxed for a moment as well as feeling a hint of amusement but collected his thoughts and started to outline her position from a legal point of view.

'Unfortunately the Law' he began, looking at her kindly 'is straight forward. Husbands own all property and assets acquired after marriage and it remains theirs after divorce.'

'Yes, I am aware of that' Mrs Briggs replied, almost sharply 'but I have a plan.' She then went on to outline her plan, and, having completed her monologue, stood up, held out her hand to shake his and left the office.

'Well I never!' Sir Richard scratched his balding head. 'Well, well, well!' He went to the window and looked down into the street. Mrs Briggs came into sight, walking briskly onto the safety zone where she stood, apparently composed, waiting for a tram.

The fact was, Madeleine Briggs was not composed at all. Once she was seated in the tram she started to get the shakes. She shifted her position on the seat away from the person beside her, leaning slightly towards the aisle. She hoped the bench wasn't shaking as well.

Once home she changed out of her going out clothes, made herself a cup of tea with a little sip of brandy on the side, sat quietly for a while and then went resolutely into one of the spare bedrooms. Opening the wardrobe she took down a large grey box, carried it into the breakfast room, placing it on the table. Inside it was full of neatly collated papers and from it she withdrew the Deed to the house. She then opened the brown paper bag she had brought home which contained a new pad of Bond paper. On the first page, using a fountain pen filled with black ink she started to write.

"I, Mathew Osborne Briggs, as sole owner, agree to gift my residence at 27 Ashton Road, including the land upon which it stands and all its contents to my wife Madeleine Helena Briggs.

Agreed to on this day, the seventeenth of October in the year nineteen hundred and twenty-one."
SignedSigned
Mathew Osborne Briggs Madeleine Helena Briggs

Witnessed by: Witnessed by:

She wrote several more identical copies, slipped them into a large envelope then went to the telephone and made the call to her husband at his place of work.

Madeleine Briggs never told anyone how she persuaded her husband Mathew to sign the papers. She never revealed who the two witnesses were. In fact, she never mentioned her husband's name again to anyone including her children. She would never grant him a divorce although, through subsequent years, he requested it several times. He in turn never paid a penny towards the upkeep of the children and, in fact, Bid and Tom never saw their father again.

HOME?

Late afternoon, on the day Bid and Tom came home to find their possessions being moved into the billiard room, Mum came into the kitchen where they were sitting at the table chatting with Eileen. She was teaching them how to make pats of butter because there were some guests coming for dinner. They would make little balls of the butter with a wet wooden implement, flattening them out and pressing a design on top. Eileen was lining up the pats in rows ready to place them in the icebox. Mum said, 'Excuse me Eileen. Come along children – we've got a job to do putting your things away...' and she turned and disappeared out into the hall.

Bid and Tom ran after her along to the billiard room. Their mother was sitting on the chesterfield which they recognised as being the one from the sitting room at home and patting it on each side of her, indicated that the children should sit there.

'Now' she said, 'we've got a great deal to discuss. We are going to live here with Grandad and Aunt Mildred and Uncle John for a while...'

Tom cut in, 'But where are we going to sleep? How long are we going to be here? What's happened to our house?' He hesitated and then said, 'Dad? What's happened to Dad?'

His mother had closed her eyes while he was interrupting and once he had finished she opened them again and said –

'There are big changes. Your father has gone away...'

Tom interrupted 'Where? Why?' and Bid said 'Stop it Tom. Let Mummy explain.'

'Your father has gone away. That's it. We are going to live here. Bid, you and I are going to sleep in this room and Tom, you've got the bedroom to yourself, next to Uncle John's room. So this is going to be our own private living room. And you've got the whole property outside to play. It's going to be lovely. Grandad says he'll teach you to play tennis and to ride the horse and he's getting each of you a bicycle. There'll be so much to do besides going to school and Grandad says you can have any of your friends to visit anytime you want to. We are going to make this our new home.

'What's happening to OUR house?' Tom asked.

'Well... I'm going to rent it out to some other people. They'll be our tenants and that will give us some money to contribute to the household expenses.'

The children sat in silence. This was a lot of information to take in but they realised that their mother had finished her explanations for now and they could see how tired she looked. And Bid, particularly, knew exactly why this was happening although she wasn't sure whether Tom knew just how serious things were where Dad was concerned. That could be left until later. There'd be lots of opportunities for her to tell him what she had seen.

SETTLED

Madeleine Briggs watched her children walk out the front gate on their way to school. Today, as a special treat she'd dressed Bid's blond curly hair into long shiny ringlets and secured them with a big white bow. The curls bounced around as Bid gave Tom a playful punch on his arm then ran ahead of him, laughing. She wore her school uniform - a navy pleated gym slip over a white shirt. Tom looked smart in his long sleeved shirt, long shorts and socks.

Once they had disappeared out of sight their mother sat down at the table, the morning sun on her back and surveyed the room. How long had they been here now? Well, over four months she calculated. She'd tried to make things as 'normal' as possible. As long as the children were happy that was all that mattered.

For her the situation was humiliating – her father having to take her and her children into his home, disrupting his life and the lives of her sister and brother.

And then the friction between her and Mildred. It was the ludicrous arrangement enforced by her sister that had led to a complete estrangement. Mildred had announced, within days of their moving in, that she wasn't going to participate in preparing 'family meals for the rest of her life'. The Briggs could eat separately in their own room and Maddy would prepare their meals when the kitchen was available.

Mildred compiled a three-meals-a-day timetable and aggressively stabbed it onto the notice board near the kitchen door where the household shopping list was recorded ready for the monthly bulk delivery from The Farmers Department Store.

The trouble between the sisters occurred when Madeleine overshot her allocated window of time in preparing the Briggs' evening meal. She was meant to be out of the kitchen, their dinners on a tray, by 6 pm sharp and it was 6.09 pm. Mildred marched into the kitchen shouting,

'What are you still doing here. You know the rules. You're so selfish...' and Maddy retaliated by turning to her sister and telling her, in a deliberately quiet measured voice which enraged her further, that she was nothing but a bad tempered nasty embittered woman.

Mildred stepped up and hit her, fist closed, on the side of her head, knocking Maddy and the dinner tray to the floor. From that moment onwards no words were exchanged between the two sisters for all of the many years that the Briggs lived in the house.

Madeleine crossed the room and sat down at her sewing machine. Out loud she said to herself, 'Oh well, now I'm just another name in the long line of her list of enemies.' After all, her sister had already fought with almost every other member of the family.

She ran several gathering stitches through the top of her client Mrs Tolmarsh's skirt in preparation for attaching it to the bodice of the dress. Mrs T had chosen a particularly ugly pattern of strange coloured squares on an exceedingly slippery silk fabric – extremely difficult to sew.

Mrs Tolmarsh was not a thin person. Rather more shapely in figure – if one wanted to be kind. A slinky pattern was not her style. The dress would certainly cling to every lump and bump. But Mrs T was a client who paid, and on time, so as far as Madeleine was concerned, she could choose any style she fancied.

She put her put her foot on the treadle and stitched on.

***

Uncle John was mowing the tennis court. It was a slow job because of his club foot and his paralysed right hand but he'd devised a method of using the machine for support. He enjoyed the rhythm of walking back and forth in the sunshine. It gave him the satisfactory feeling that he was making a contribution to the household.

He was feeling happy. Before the arrival of his sister and his niece and nephew, when he really thought about it, his life had been lonely. Father was good to him but he was here and there on his own business.

John Walsh had become wealthy when he had sold his substantial retail emporium which occupied a prime location in the city. He had invested his money wisely in property – retail, residential and commercial – and spent a lot of time managing his investments. On Fridays he drove into the city to collect the rents.

Yes – the arrival of the Briggs had made Uncle John feel happy. Now there was always activity around the house when the children weren't at school. And on weekends, other children would visit. And having Maddy in the house was company as well. Mildred had never been company. She always seemed to be in a bad temper and would complain that he was in the way, so he'd spend most of his time in his bedroom, except at mealtimes.

Going to the pictures on Fridays was Uncle John's only independent outing of the week. He'd take the tram into the city, always sitting in exactly the same theatre seat. On Thursday nights he'd visit the Briggs' room to find out what kind of lollies Bid and Tom would like him to bring home for them. They'd take ages to decide and would receive their weekly delivery on Saturday mornings in their own separate miniature brown paper bags.

It was getting hot and just as he was about to take a break, leaning against the big roller, John heard his father's car take the turn into the gate with a squeal and speed up the driveway on the other side of the house. The dogs, Trooper and Flop, jumped out of the car and came racing across the tennis court to greet him.

They were Grandad's dogs. Trooper was an Australian Kelpie, tan in colour, lean and very intelligent. Flop had arrived with the Briggs but had now decided he was also Grandad's dog. He was a black cocker spaniel, silly but very loveable. They jumped and circled around him, their tongues lolling and tails wagging until Uncle John stood up and herded them back towards the house.

***

Bid and her mother were busy sewing. Bid was really keen to learn to make her own clothes. She was struggling a bit with the Singer as this was her first try, the main problem being that she really had to stretch her legs to reach the treadle. But Mummy was a good teacher – very patient.

'Whoops-a-daisy!' Bid had run into another snag in the operation of the machine. She glanced up to ask her mother for help. Madeleine Briggs was sitting in one of the armchairs just staring out the bay window – at nothing it seemed.

'She's depressed' Bid thought. 'I know that.'

Even at the young age of nine years Bid could sense what a strain everything was for her mother. Unable to live in her own home and now, only in one room. Having to dodge Aunt Mildred due to the estrangement. It was all Aunt Mildred's fault, she was such a bad tempered old grump. She had made it very clear that having her sister and her two children turn up to live in the house was a big blow to her. She made it obvious that she resented it deeply.

Mummy was trying to make everything seem as normal as possible but Bid knew she felt her situation very badly. She was proud and being separated from her husband left her in an isolated position socially. She didn't really seem to have any friends or outside interests. She did lots of sewing, making clothes for other people, but sometimes these people didn't pay. Grandad paid for everything and Mummy didn't really have any actual money in her purse to be independent and go shopping and buy nice things. Bid sensed she was lonely and she knew her mother was ashamed of what had happened.

However, Bid had to admit that for her and Tom, things were really rather good. True – she didn't have her own bedroom anymore but all the advantages of living on a large property with lots to do made them popular with their school friends. Grandad made them feel so welcome, thinking up all kinds of activities. He taught them how to plant vegies in the kitchen garden, feed the beautiful coloured birds in the aviary, feed the chooks and collect the eggs. It was fun.

On wet days Grandad would bring out the horse and trap to drive them to school. The horse was a big chestnut mare named Madge. Taking Madge out seemed to make Grandad feel contented as he would whistle as they trotted along. Bid and Tom loved Grandad's well-meaning practice of taking them to school when it was raining. He was a fantastic storyteller and would make up all kinds of unbelievable tales, many of which featured Madge's imaginary exploits like jumping over trams. The only snag about taking the trap when it was raining was that there was no roof so the children were protected by a heavy leather cover which was rolled up to their necks, but their heads just had their hats. Bid and Tom could never fathom why Grandad didn't take them in the Wolesley.

CRISIS

1922

It was a warm Friday in Autumn and Tom and Bid were down in the orchard. By now the Briggs had been living at Coronation Road for well over a year. Before he set off to the city to collect the rents Grandad had given them instructions (once they arrived home from school) to go and pick apples and he was very specific about which varieties.

'After all this time she still won't call me Bid when everyone else does. She always calls me Louise although one day, when she was telling me off, she did call me A Little Biddy. I think she's just a very unhappy person.' Bid stretched up to grab a Cox's Orange that was just out of reach.

'Who?' Tom had climbed up into a tree and was shaking the branches. Granny Smiths were bouncing around as they hit the grass.

'You shouldn't be doing that – they'll get bruised – Aunt Mildred, stupid.'

'Holy Moly! Aunt Dread you mean' snorted Tom. 'She's a regular nightmare.'

By now, approaching his thirteenth birthday, Tom had been the recipient of numerous confrontations with Mildred because he was cocky and defiant. He'd received quite a few whacks around the head and on one occasion she had taken him by the scruff of the neck, opened the kitchen door and thrown him out onto the back porch. He seriously hated her.

'Y'know she drinks.'

'Drinks? What do you mean?'

'Gin' Tom nodded. 'I snooped one day when she was out.'

'You mean you went into her room...?'

'Yep.' Triumphantly. 'She had the bottles hidden in the back of her wardrobe.'

He gave a branch another shake.

'I think that'll do. That's enough.'

Tom had started to climb down the tree when Trooper came racing down the slope towards them barking. Following him, ears blowing back, tongue out and yelping, came Flop. The two dogs started jumping around barking and whining and Trooper kept running up the hill towards the house, stopping and looking back at them.

'Somethings going on – c'mon.' Tom started to follow the dogs, Bid following him lugging the basketful of apples.

They hurried along behind the stable buildings and out into the back yard.

Uncle John was lying on the ground, all sort of crumpled up, on his side, as if he was sleeping. Blood was oozing out of one of his ears. Aunt Mildred was pacing back and forth near him, hands on her hips, looking down and then around as if she was expecting someone or something.

'What's happened?' The two children circled Uncle John and Bid crumpled down beside him to stroke the side of his head saying 'Uncle John! What's wrong? What happened?'

'Tom said 'Have you called the doctor?' Aunt Mildred glared at him.

'She's drunk' Tom thought, glaring back.

He raced into the house yelling 'Mum! Mum!' and she came out of their room and began running towards him along the hall. As she ran, Tom was shouting at her. 'Call the Doctor Mum! Call the Doctor! It's Uncle John...!'

She ran outside, knelt down and felt her brother's pulse.

'It'll take too long for the Doctor to come. We need to get him to the hospital' She paused and then exclaimed 'But Father's in town...!'

Tom yelled 'We could take the trap! I know how to harness Madge. Grandad taught me.' He raced into the horse's stall and led her out.

'I'll help' Mum said. 'I can manage the trap.'

She glanced around. 'You stay beside Uncle John, Bid – can you do that?' and as Bid nodded Mum said "But where's Mildred? *Mildred?*' she shouted. 'Oh for heaven's sake! Go and find Eileen, Bid. Hurry!'

Together they managed to gently lift Uncle John into the trap – after all, he wasn't very heavy. He lay on the floor on top of Bid's pink silk eiderdown under a blanket which she had tenderly placed over him. Eileen ran back inside and fetched a pillow for his head.

'To make you more comfy' she said as if he could hear her.

The flow of blood had stopped. Uncle John lay as if he was all folded up, his eyes closed, his poor right hand curled up in its strange way, one heavy built-up boot still on his club foot. Bid began to cry. Tom crouched down with his hand on his uncle's shoulder as if to assure him that he was in charge.

'He looks so frail' Tom thought. 'Is he dead?' An uncomfortable lump was rising up in his throat. For the first time in his life he wished he wasn't a boy so he could cry. Mum was amazing! She was in charge. Look how she was marshalling everyone.

'Lock the dogs in the house Eileen. You come with us. We all need to go together.' Mum looked around. 'Where on earth is Mildred?'

Tom thought. 'Hopefully The Dread is dead.' He couldn't help but feel the inappropriate semblance of a chuckle developing to replace the lump in his throat.

They eased along the driveway and once out onto the road, set off at a trot, Madge's long chestnut tail swinging reassuringly in front of them, her haunches moving rhythmically back and forth as if she knew this outing was important.

Tom turned his head. Mum was sitting up beside him, so straight, holding the reins in a business-like manner. Every now and then she'd gently brush the reins across Madge's back and say, in an affectionate way 'That's right Madge – good old girl. You'll get him there safely.'

Tom turned to look at Bid and Eileen sitting on the seat behind. They were like a guard of honour, watching over Uncle John. For some unknown reason, despite the fact that he sensed tragedy ahead, he felt secure in the knowledge that they were a family. That Grandad would be waiting for them once they arrived at the hospital. That he would know what to do and that there was Team Work ahead.

He turned and looked forward.

A 21ˢᵗ CENTURY PRILGRIM'S PROGRESS

They were bowling down the M-1 now. Where was the next stop? Hannah couldn't be bothered looking up the itinerary. The whole of England was flashing past. York one day. Chatsworth another. Onto the coach. Off the coach. The little huddle of mostly grey and balding heads were herded through the "Points of Interest", clustering around the tour guide, straining to hear what he or she was saying.

Nothing like her first trip to England back in '77 when she'd toured with Marcus. They'd pottered. Hannah had the guidebook and they'd only got lost once when they went three times round Exeter. But they'd ambled through sunken lanes between walls of petalled snow – Queen Anne's lace and hawthorn. If they saw a sign that said "Willow Under the Wallow" or "Saxon Ruins" or suchlike, they'd make an impulsive detour and just *go there*!

They had driven out of London to Bath where they stayed on the Royal Terrace would you believe! In an apartment lent by one of their English friends. They'd strolled into town that first evening. It was May Day and the Morris Dancers were out. The Assembly Rooms were lit with candles and they sat and enjoyed a concert. They spent three days there, seeing everything, taking their time and then they set off down into the West Country – exploring at leisure. Then onwards up to the Lake District for several days and back to London via York and Chatsworth. A whole two weeks of wandering at will, so what was she doing on this coach – retracing steps?

Well, it was the family's fault. They had been horrified when Hannah announced that for her 82nd birthday she wanted to make her final trip to England, on her own and in Business Class into the bargain, and that she specifically wanted to go back to Kent. Her great grandparents had emigrated to New Zealand from there in 1862. But it was Canterbury Cathedral she felt she had to see one last time. The urge was so great when she let herself seriously think about it that she'd get a lump in her throat. Ridiculous really but it was all to do with her roots. Born in the Antipodes, nonetheless, the essence of her belonged there – in Kent. Ancestral records from 1500 placed her family in locations with ancient names like Lydd, St-Mary-in-the-Marsh, Broadstairs and Canterbury.

Finally the family had reluctantly agreed provided she joined a tour. By the time she had been widowed and was progressing at what seemed like a cracking pace through her seventies, Hannah had sworn she'd never do another guided tour in her life! She hated being theoretically trapped with strangers. By the time she'd been with them for what seemed aeons she couldn't endure another moment and to be fair, they probably felt the same about her.

Where were they going next? Ah yes ... Salisbury. Well, Salisbury was lovely but no doubt they'd dash through the Cathedral in half an hour max and then be back on the bus.

Oh! They were arriving. The party trailed into the hotel lobby. Room keys were distributed.

In her room Hannah sat down on the bed and suddenly the overwhelming conviction that she must escape landed on her with such an impact that she felt quite shaken by it. She stared at her suitcase, still locked, its contents undisturbed. She hadn't even taken off her jacket. She fished around in the pocket for her iPhone and Googled "Hire Car Companies". Several wouldn't take her. At 82 she was uninsurable. During one enquiry she yelled at the schoolgirl voice on the other end. 'What's age got to do with it?' Eventually she was successful but not without paying a hefty additional insurance supplement with a softener that they would deliver the car to the hotel for her.

It was a merry little two door vehicle, bright red with a hatch back. Quite uplifting really! 'Would you like me to set the GPS for you?' enquired the hire car man, loading her suitcase into the boot. 'Sure' Hannah replied. She didn't bother to tell him she knew how to organise it on her phone. She drove him back to the hire car place. His knuckles were white as he gripped the sill of the passenger door. 'Thanks a lot' he said, bolting back into the office.

Hannah, ignoring the GPS that he had set for Canterbury, used the exquisitely soaring spire as a guide to Salisbury Cathedral. She parked and strolled across the green to the main door. She entered. Utter beauty! She wandered. She sat in a pew and drank in the glorious windows. She visited Lady Katherine Grey's tomb. She stood before the faceless clock. 1386! How *wonderful*! Two hours' later she was on the road, heading for Canterbury.

It was quite late when she arrived so she booked into a private hotel near the Cathedral. By this time her phone was going bonkers – tour company and family back home trying to trace her whereabouts. She texted. "AWOL. Sorry! I'm just fine. Touring independently. Don't worry. Will keep in touch."

Hannah entered Canterbury Cathedral. It soared, this monumental masterpiece. Unbearable emotion welled up. After a thousand years here it still stood, the divine destination of the early pilgrims who, 800 years ago had walked through the mud of endless towns and villages to worship and honour Thomas á Becket. The modest candle was there on the flagstones, its steadfast flame marking his violent demise.

She sat, thinking of Marcus. She wandered in awe, relishing her independence. Other people's footsteps and voices surrounded her in that noble space, softly echoing the shuffling millions that had preceded them from the Middle Ages of Time. Her ancestral family had been amongst them. She belonged. She was fulfilled.

Tomorrow? She'd head for Cornwall via all those ancestral towns and with a delightful detour to Sissinghurst.

WAITING FOR THE TRAIN

The man – a smooth looking man – sat on a seat on the railway platform. He was early. Far too early and this made him irritable. He was a person who hated wasting a minute, who always had to feel productive. He couldn't stand going to bed without the conclusion that he had achieved something during the day.

'Yes... what a waste of time this is' he reflected as he opened his newspaper and summarily scanned a few pages. But somehow none of the headlines, negative as usual, grabbed his attention. He carelessly folded the paper, dumped it on the seat beside him and glanced around.

People were standing along the platform waiting for earlier trains. Most were looking down at their phones – scrolling, scrolling. What on earth were they looking at? Irritation rose again. 'This vapid world' he muttered.

A train slid in and he watched passengers disembarking. Judgementally he scanned the crowd. What a depressing looking mob! Grumpy faces, no eye contact, black clothing with few exceptions. Many in a hurry, ploughing their way through the waiting passengers with no regard for the right of others to their piece of space. The grumpies got off and the waiting grumpies got on – except for a couple of elderly ladies. Wisely they had waited for the crowd to clear before disembarking and now they were carefully stepping across between the carriage and the platform.

'ere Flo. 'ang onto me arm. It's tricky. Remember the time I fell flat on me face getting orf the Piccadilly Line? Cor... that was a to do if ever there was one. The ambos were a treat. 'ad me parcelled up and into St George's before I could say 'Hoot'. Tha' ankle's been wonky ever since.'

A young man, getting on, impatiently elbowed them aside and the two friends, linked together, staggered and wobbled but remained upright.

'Well! Typical! Rude bastard! I don't know. The world's gone to pot Flo - doncha think?'

'Forget 'em' Flo replied as they toddled off towards the exit, hunched over, taking short steps in their practical sneakers and woollen beanies, arm in arm, chatting away. Short in stature, enveloped in their padded jackets, their departing backs made them resemble a couple of miniature puffballs on legs each with a fluffy blue or orange oversized cherry on top.

'Well, they're a happy pair.' The observer felt a vague feeling of – what? Self-pity? How many close friends did he have? Well, none if he was to be brutally honest. He imagined these two women had been friends for a long time and it would be a guess that they lived modestly and frugally. How old would they be? Late seventies at least. Eighties? Widows? They'd have seen a lot. They'd probably had tough lives. And then he thought 'But it seems that women make and keep far more friends than men do.'

He adjusted his position on the wooden bench, checking it for pigeon droppings. He stood up and fastidiously investigated the backside of his suit then sat down again, crossing his legs and adjusting his briefcase. He checked his phone and texted his client's secretary to confirm he was coming by train and that he'd phone when the train was approaching Lewes so they could send the car. As a barrister it was unusual for him to visit a client but he'd been Pullson's lawyer for getting on thirty years so it was the least he could do to pay him a visit as the fellow was virtually an invalid now and well on into his eighties. This would be the third visit he'd made to change The Will. The old boy seemed to be continually moving legatees around – family members who had fallen in or out of favour. The last time he'd been there Pullson had said 'Well Jarratt. I've had it with the lot of 'em. I'm giving consideration to a large number of charities at present. I'll get you back when I've decided.'

A woman with a young toddler in a stroller bumped into the man's crossed leg as she passed. She threw an offhand 'Sorry' back over her shoulder as she manoeuvred through the crowd. The baby, sitting up, stared at the man and suddenly bestowed a beaming smile. He leant forward with his arms positioned straight on his leggings as if he had something confidential to say. His cheeks were red which made the tiny baby teeth inside the smile appear exceptionally white. He was wearing a red beanie with an enormous pompom on top. 'Da Da' he said and, as he disappeared amongst the sea of legs, he leant his head on the side of the stroller and peeped, keeping his eyes and the smile still fixed on the man until they were out of sight.

Something huge welled up – a sort of terror that made the man feel he might begin to weep. He couldn't believe the sudden emotion; it was so many years. How old would Anton be now? Forty-six? Forty-seven? Somewhere in the States? Married? Children? Job? Mortgage? He didn't have any idea. She'd just up and left him when the boy was only 5 years' old. Just disappeared – never to be heard of again. Had it been today in this world of advanced technology he'd have been able to trace them. It wasn't as if he hadn't tried. Now it was so long ago. So long that he'd been waiting – forever fruitlessly hopeful.

The newspaper rustled and shuffled on the bench and he turned to discover a young girl, late teens possibly, had swept the paper onto the ground. Her head was resting on the back of the seat and her body, ramrod straight, stretched out to long thin bare legs, crossed, with the feet, in an incongruously huge pair of trainers, balancing on one heel on the ground. She was wearing a miniscule pair of denim shorts, frayed around the hem topped by some sort of colourful knitted wrap which enveloped her entire upper body. Her head, emerging from the top of this tentlike garment was small and refined with long straight blond hair parted down the middle and hanging in drab curtains on either side of her face. She glanced briefly at him. Her face was wan with an expression that was vaguely aggressive, but her eyes were beautiful – large and a strangely pale indistinguishable colour.

'Hey'... she said, and looked away immediately.

'Hello' Jarratt responded stiffly.

The girl continued to stare into the distance as if she was completely alone and the constant activity on the platform didn't exist.

Jarratt checked the time. Two minutes. At last! He rose, picking up his briefcase. The train appeared around the bend amongst the multitude of lines and crept slowly into the station. He walked forward and joined other passengers. The engine was edging towards him and then he felt himself shoved on his shoulder so that he staggered to one side. There was a flash of colour. The girl was running, thrusting people left and right and then she jumped. There was a thud. The train stopped. People screamed and it was as if a huge sigh moved through the crowd – a wave of despair and then a whirlpool formed as people surged forward or recoiled. The train reversed ever so slightly. Jarratt could see the driver's face – an older man. Later, when he allowed himself recall, he couldn't bear to remember the expression on that face.

He stepped to the edge of the platform. An unbelievably small pile of vivid colours lay on the lines like a load of washing dumped from a basket. Sirens were wailing. He turned away. Paramedics were arriving. Police took his statement.

At Lewes the driver was waiting. Jarratt had advised that he was running late. He and Pullson conducted their business then chatted over a late lunch and some very superior wine. And then, still in shock, while he was sitting in First Class watching the East Sussex countryside slide by, he made a phone call to the police.

'I'm a witness to the train accident at Victoria Station this morning. I made a statement. Can you connect me with the attending officer?'

A moment passed then a man's voice said 'Detective Brockman.'

'Yes – thank you. My name's Rupert Jarratt. I gave a witness statement at Victoria Station this morning...

'Yes, yes' the voice interrupted.

'Have you identified the girl?'

'We have.'

'Are you permitted to give me her name? Just a courtesy, you know – should her family at some stage want any information. I would have been the last person to speak to her.'

'Yes Sir. Call back in a day or two. This is a bit premature. The family have been notified. In the United States' he added.

After an appropriate length of time Jarratt called the detective again. He was provided with the family's contact details and her name.

Isobella Jarratt.

SPRING RAIN

What was that? Plop! Plop! Two big plops on the iron roof. Could it be? Could it **really** be? Silence – then patter patter.

Rain? Oh please let it be rain. It stopped. It was teasing her.

The sky was cloudy and the day had been humid, now it was cold. She went to bed and lay there listening. There it was again! Patter patter. And the gentle steady sound of little raindrops on the roof. How wonderful!

'Don't stop! **Please** don't stop!'

Then it got down to business and set to in a steady musical rhythm. She could hear water overflowing from the gutters.

Out of bed she sprang, grabbing an umbrella, running out into the night garden. The rain beat on the umbrella straight and true. The Spring garden reached up its arms and welcomed the rain. The huge white camellia flowers were shining out like soft orbs in the darkness. The heads of the daffodils, so perky in the sun of the afternoon, were bowing down now, weighted with water but glowing yellow in the gloom. All the plants in the garden lifted their leaves as the dusty drought-filled day was washed away. Even the bare branches of the still leafless deciduous trees seemed to lift their limbs in thanks as their roots drank and drank.

Oh how beautiful it was. 'Please stay!'

She looked up at the dark starless sky. 'Don't stop!'

She went inside and got back into bed ... listening. She was a very small child back in her grandmother's dear old house, beneath the iron roof, below the rosy frieze on the top of the bedroom wall, snuggled down under the shiny pink silk eiderdown with just her little nose peeking out, listening to the comforting sound of the rain – pattering, beating, never stopping. She remembered she would lie there listening and singing a poem quietly to herself. To her own made up tune.

> *"The rain is raining all around*
> *It falls on field and tree*
> *It rains on the umbrellas here*
> *And on the ships at sea".*

Whose poem was that? Ah yes! Robert Louis Stevenson.
She slept.

SETH AND SARAH

'Further! Further! To the right! No – back a bit.' Aunty Sarah was flapping her hands with their long pink nails up and down like a deranged seal. Seth was dragging the poles and the net around on the sand in a resigned manner. God she was embarrassing! Mum always said she was a bit nutty. But he mustn't think about Mum…

He looked up at the beach house. No sign of the others. Couldn't she wait until the rest of them came down? Honestly this whole performance was utterly futile until they came to help. But Sarah – she insisted that he call her "Sarah" so perhaps she thought being called "Aunty" would make people think she was old – which of course she was. Look at her! Completely weird. All that long tossing blond hair and the big dangly earrings. The brief pink shorts looked stupid stretched over her fat bottom above her chunky short legs and her top kept riding up leaving a gap with a roll of fat exposed. Totally embarrassing! She had masses of bright coloured bracelets on including the ones young people wear messaging about the environment and the oceans.

What a contrast to Mum who never wore makeup, who wasn't at all interested in fashion, who had once been a hippy apparently. He had been born in India to some unknown dude in an ashram and he'd been named Seth after Vikram Seth, an author who Mum admired. All that Mum had ever told him about his dad was that he was an American and "A good person" and that was it!

Sarah was a good person. No doubt about that. The way she had taken over after Mum. There was no hesitation from the very moment The Horror happened. She seemed to completely understand how he felt. That he wanted to be hugged but that he couldn't. That he wanted to cry, but he couldn't. He was *so* angry. All he wanted to do was disappear forever. Curl up in a secret place and stay there until he was dead too ... with Mum. So Sarah just got down to supervising the practicalities like packing up all his stuff – his clothes and all the things in his room – the banners and posters and laptop and all the rest. Everything was moved to his own room at his cousins' house and they set it up to look like his room at Mum's. Which was really cool of them but he wasn't sure about it. But that was okay because Sarah said, 'You might not be happy with this Seth so move your things around once you've settled in. We can paint it another colour if you like. Take your time.'

He scanned the beach. Where *were* they? God he felt awful! Desperate. He stood there looking pathetic, shoulders slumped, the beach volleyball paraphernalia strewn around his feet while Sarah fluffed around. Her boobs were in constant movement partially exposed by the V-neck of her t-shirt. Bummer! There were some people walking towards them and there she went, running up to them, arms waving, bracelets jingling, everything bouncing around.

'Oh would you?' She was being flirty to the man. 'You *are* a doll.' And then, just as the good-natured man was approaching Seth to help, the rest of them came bounding down the cliff steps – Uncle Hugh and Mia, Tom and Brad. Surprisingly that loser Giles was slouching reluctantly after them. He was sixteen and had entered into Teenage Retirement. Seth had overheard Uncle Hugh say this to Sarah when she was complaining about Giles's rude offhand behaviour.

'He'll work his way through it. We just need to get him out the other side intact.'

So Sarah, who was generally pretty houseproud, stopped even entering Giles' room and as Giles was in Teenage Retirement he kept his door locked, just managing to dump some washing in the laundry occasionally. He hardly ever talked and did smell a bit at times – sort of stuffy. Seth seldom heard him in the shower. One day when Giles was out Seth noticed he had left his door slightly ajar, so he pushed it a little and poked his head around the crack to have a look. It sure was stuffy! The bed was invisible under numerous grimy pillows with no pillowcases and a yucky old doona with no cover on it and so was the floor as there was so much stuff dropped on it – jeans, underwear, books, sneakers, a puffer jacket, empty cans and used coffee mugs. He had a play station in there and a TV and there was a desk with a laptop on it. But boy, it sure was a smelly crash site!

Seth had never got to see Mum. They said it was best not. He wanted to and then, because he was frightened about how she might look – like – dead, he really didn't. But he felt he *should*. It was all so confusing. God he felt awful! But the game was underway now and everyone was tearing around like lunatics and hurling themselves onto the sand and whooping and cheering and he tried to join in with their mood but boy it was difficult.

"Going through the motions". He'd read that phrase somewhere. Perhaps they were talking about a zombie. He wasn't sure how zombies felt but he related to them because they *looked* the way he felt. Lumbering and plodding and depressed. His chest was heavy all the time, short of leaden and achy, he had a permanent pain in his stomach and his brain was reduced to a paralysed nothingness. 'Thanks God.' He sent a mental thumbs up just in case God *did* exist because Christmas meant school holidays had started so he didn't have to try to use his mushy brain.

Christmas! How could she do it at Christmas? Apparently lots of people got depressed at Christmas. It was quite common. He'd overheard this discussion when he was snooping after all the kids had gone to bed and Sarah and Uncle Hugh were talking very quietly down in the family room. Seth did a lot of snooping whenever it was opportune. He needed to gather information somehow – to understand about Mum. He understood that everyone was trying to protect him but he needed to know why. *Why* had she done it? How had she done it? Fearful of the answer he almost preferred not to know.

But why would she have chosen to leave him? This was the worst thing. They'd got on pretty well on the whole, the two of them, or so he'd thought. So what could he have done to make her want to top herself? He felt his heart was breaking. He'd complied with her lifestyle which meant she was out a lot. He never whinged or asked her why or where she'd been. He was thirteen now and could fend for himself but it *was* a bit lonely at times and he was totally over Maccas and Kentucky Fried. She'd loaded a debit card app on his phone so he could buy meals on the nights she was out. Sometimes she'd leave him a note but often she didn't. He just had to go with the flow.

Aunty Sarah kept in touch. His mobile would ring – always after school.

'Just checking on you both' she'd say pointedly and when he'd tell her Mum wasn't there she'd pause for a moment before she'd say, sort of forcefully, *'Right!* Come and have dinner then – see you soon' and Seth would ride his bike over to their place, remembering to take his school gear and his homework, just in case they insisted he stay the night which happened more often than not. It was like his alternative home when he really thought about it.

And he had company there, with his cousins. They were pretty good on the whole apart from Giles. The twins, Tom and Brad were twelve years' old and generally pretty mature for their age. The three of them played cricket together and hung out so that was all good. Mia was a bit of a pain at times being only nine. She had a gross pink room with a crowd of anorexic Barbies and big posters of soppy girly movies but generally she was okay and was usually busy giggling away in there with her immature school friends. And Uncle Hugh – well he was awesome. He owned some humungous business and seemed to go overseas quite a lot but when he was at home he seemed to forget about his big job and was great company and good at giving advice, that is, if you happened to ask for it. He was a terrific Dad and he *really* loved Sarah.

Mum seemed to know a lot of people but he rarely got to meet them except when occasionally he'd get up in the morning and there'd be some dude in the kitchen making coffee. This was very unsettling because most of them ignored him and made him feel it was their place and he was just an irritating visitor. They looked sort of young compared to Mum and usually had beards and long hair and wore t-shirts with messages on them but why were they farting around at Mum's place? They should be out doing something productive. And what did Mum do? Frankly he had no idea. On the few occasions he plucked up courage to ask her what her job was she was very vague and muttered something about "Research" and she seemed to be away more often than at home.

When the detectives talked to him they asked him a lot of questions about Mum and he was pretty useless actually. He was nervous and puzzled until Uncle Hugh explained in his usual reasonable way that this was the normal procedure when there was a death, unless the person died of an illness. But a few days later he was beginning to feel suspicious because he realised there had been no talk of a funeral. Didn't people who died usually have a funeral a short time after – like – a week or so? He decided to pluck up courage and ask Sarah. The opportunity presented itself one wet morning when she was doing the school drop off so once they were alone he got straight to the point.

'Sarah? When's Mum going to have her funeral?'

She turned her head to look at him briefly and then back to the road. He felt uneasy because she hesitated and he sensed she was trying to get her words sorted. Finally she said, 'Well dear, the police are just doing their job and there's a thing called a Coroner's Report so once all that is completed and we receive the Death Certificate we'll plan a wonderful funeral for Rachel.'

She was looking a bit upset, sort of teary, so Seth didn't ask anything else. He just started fiddling with his backpack getting it sorted so he could leap out of the car when they got to school and shoot inside. They stopped and he started to open the door but at the same time he looked back at Sarah and she was really crying. He lunged across the passenger seat and planted a big kiss on her cheek.

This made her cry even more, so, amazed that he had even done such a thing and unable to cope, he shot out of the car and dashed through the rain.

It had been difficult going to school so soon after the news of The Horror but Sarah and Uncle Hugh persuaded him that it would be better to continue his usual routine. All the kids were really nice to him, y'know, sympathetic. Most of them didn't actually *say* anything, just super friendly but every now and then one of the guys would say 'Sorry about that mate' in a very grow-up sort of way and give him a friendly pat on the back. He understood. What do you say when someone's mother has suddenly died and you are thirteen years old. Fortunately, he only had to endure their kindnesses for a week or so and then, relief, the school holidays began.

So now, despite things not having been sorted out for Mum, it was announced they were moving to the beach house. Waiheke was okay – great house – great location – but it had been better back in Auckland where somehow he felt nearer to Mum and he had his own room. On the car ferry he'd been given the bad news that he would be sharing with Giles. Thinking of Giles' room in Auckland this definitely seemed a low point but once they arrived it wasn't too bad as they were in the huge playroom down in the basement so he got himself hunkered down on the far side of the room and pushed his bed near the windows so he could look out at the sea and get fresh air.

Giles was his usual uncommunicative self the first few days but one night when he came down he sat on his bed which was already looking distinctly skanky and stared across at Seth who was lying down scrolling his phone.

'You okay?' he asked.

'Yeah…' Seth looked up. He honestly didn't have a clue how to answer.

'It's pretty fuckin' creepy – what's happened to your Mum,' Giles continued, pushing back his long greasy hair. 'So I was just wonderin' what you think about it – y'know – like how you're coping.'

'What do you mean?' Seth responded. A great surge of fear was rising up making his head burn.

'Well, not knowing what happened 'xactly. Y'know – trying to find out who did it.'

'Did *what*? Wadda y'mean?' The fear was producing a feeling that his head was going to burst at any moment but Giles just continued to stare at him so he said, '**She** did it but they haven't told me how yet. I suppose they think I can't take it. Yet.' He added miserably. He had the most appalling feeling he was going to start blubbering and in front of, of all people, this jerk Giles. Why was he saying these things? Seth felt that any moment he might throw up.

And then suddenly, out of all his misery and confusion there welled up the most terrifying feeling of utter rage. What did Giles know? What did his aunt and uncle know that they weren't telling him? She was his *mother!* He flung his phone at Giles and raced upstairs. Sarah and Uncle Hugh were sitting out on the terrace. He burst through the open glass doors and screamed at them.

'What's going on? What haven't you told me? Why are you leaving me out? **She's my mother!'**

Sarah ran towards him but he pushed her so violently that she fell against a chair. He continued to scream at them hysterically – sobbing, unhinged – hurling his body around the terrace. All the grief and shame and frustration and the sense of loss and the conviction that he must keep control of his feelings was ejected with such force that his head was spinning and he ended up clinging to the terrace railing so he wouldn't fall over.

By now his aunt and uncle were circling in a protective way in case he hurt himself and all the kids, including Giles, had appeared, clustering together behind the glass doors. Uncle Hugh, usually such a calm bloke, yelled at them to go back to their rooms which, shocked at his uncharacteristic aggression, they did. He was sweating and red in the face and looking really distressed as he turned back and circled his nephew saying, 'It's okay son, it's okay'.

Sarah was crying and moaning

'Oh Seth, Seth! You poor love. We're sorry. Truly. Just sit down for a moment while I get you something to drink and … and we'll explain.

Seth staggered over to the sofa and slumped down, spent and exhausted, taking great gasps of air. Sarah returned with a long glass containing what looked to be lemonade and a lot of ice cubes but when he took a sip it wasn't lemonade, it was tonic water and after he'd taken a few big gulps something really nice started to happen in his stomach. It suddenly felt comfortable and settled and Sarah smiled at him and said, 'I put a drop of vodka in there. It'll help you. I hope that's okay?' And Seth, calmer now, nodded miserably and said, 'Thanks Aunt.' And then 'Sorry.'

The three of them sat in silence for a while looking at the sea. It looked black and oily in the darkness with a brilliant slash of rippling light where the bright moon was throwing down its reflection. Uncle Hugh said, 'Do you want to talk now Seth?' and Seth nodded. He felt calm now, almost contented which was weird. It must be the booze working. Uncle Hugh continued, 'We are very sorry we have made you feel left out. We thought we were doing the right thing because the truth is, we still haven't got any final confirmation ourselves about what has really happened. The fact is the police have told us they don't believe your mother killed herself. They say there definitely are suspicious circumstances and that they are sure that Rachel was killed by someone else.'

Seth started to shiver. The fear was overwhelming but this time it was accompanied by a feeling of stultifying shock. What Uncle Hugh was actually saying was that Mum might have been murdered! Then he suddenly thought, if this were to be true and Mum hadn't killed herself, well, then, it couldn't have been his fault – could it? He looked at his aunt and uncle. Sarah was staring at him with such love. Tears were covering her cheeks and she hid her face in her hands. Her shoulders began shaking violently and Seth suddenly remembered that, consumed by his own misery, he had completely overlooked the fact that Mum had been her sister.

He stood up. Boy, he felt a bit legless! He walked unsteadily over to Aunty Sarah. He knelt down and put his arms around her soft comfy waist. He laid his head against her chest. Sarah wrapped her arms around him and rocked him back and forth. And then, at last, releasing from its depths his utter grief, Seth cried.

LUCIFER

Now, I'd like to clear something up right from the start. I am a Cat. I am a Lucky Cat because I am adopted. It would be a shock to My Humans if they were to know how much I understand about their behaviour; that I eavesdrop when they are talking; that I recognise their noises.

My First Humans lived in a shanty high up on the hillsides of Hong Kong. When the summer rains came, a big landslide of mud arrived. Being a Lucky Cat, I was cowering up in a tree at the time and watched my home and the other Humans' homes slide down the steep slope until the mud buried everything, including my First Humans. After the rain stopped I crept down the tree trunk. There was so much deep wet mud that I had to carefully choose where to place my paws. At last, when I got to the bottom of the hill I was a brown Cat rather than a white one. I started to call out, searching for my First Humans. I cried and cried. I never found them.

I wandered around searching for many days. I was so tired. I slept where I could find a dry place. I caught rats and carried them underneath a big building where there were cars. It was dry in there and I learnt that cars that had only recently parked were the warmest place to be. I would crouch underneath them and eat my rat and curl up and sleep when I could. It took me days to clean off the mud. My neck was so painful once I had finished all that licking but my fur was still matted and a strange burnt colour.

One day I was slinking along beside a wall. I was in familiar territory as my First Humans had worked there. They sold Human food. Lots of Humans crowded up and down the steep steps. I heard Humans say that many of them were Tourists and they liked to visit this place called Ladder Street. These Tourist Humans had helped my First Humans make money.

Suddenly two Humans were looking at me and Big Human said, 'Look at that poor Cat! How sad. It's obviously a stray.'

The Little Human said, 'We should take it home' and suddenly scooped me up.

Big Human said, 'Don't be ridiculous. Put it down. It'll have all kinds of diseases and fleas.'

So I began to purr. I was very weak but I put all my energy into it. That did the trick.

Little Human said, 'Oh it's purring! Poor little love.'

They got on a tram in Queen's Road and then got off again a few stops along. I kept very still. I sensed these Humans were not tourists. They knew how to get around. I didn't struggle. I sensed I was onto a good thing and I was right. Cats know things.

Then my New Humans got on the Peak Tram and got off at The Mid-Levels. They lived in a big building quite near to where I had ended up in the mud. Inside it was warm and dry and soft under my paws with many comfy places to jump up on and sleep. I'd never seen anything so wonderful! But, after all, I *am* a Lucky Cat.

The only bad thing they did to me was put me into some warm water. They rubbed my fur with something. Bad. Then they put me in some more warm water and wrapped me up in something soft.

They rubbed me and unwrapped me and Little Human said, 'Oh how beautiful! It's pure white! It's gorgeous! We have to adopt it!'

Big Human said nothing.

'What'll we call it?' said Little Human.

'Looks like trouble to me, but if you're going to adopt it, I think... Lucifer.'

***

My Adopted Humans were good to me. I was so happy. They went away a lot but there was another Human who lived with them who was very busy all the time so it didn't give me much attention. But it did feed me. That was the priority so I didn't bother with it either. I didn't rub against its legs or make myself look adorable. I just slept a lot.

One day when My Adopted Humans were away a huge wind started up. It was very bad. I heard it saying 'Typhoon'. I was on my Adopted Humans' sleeping place. It began to rock and shudder and there were rumbles and then suddenly I was buried. My new home fell on me. It was black and I was trapped in dust and heavy grey rubble. I could hear The Other Human calling out but I couldn't escape. After a long time it stopped. I scratched the grey rocks until I had no claws left. My tail was broken. I was a Trapped Cat. I was so exhausted I just lay there. I knew I would eventually be dead. Buried like my First Humans. I was no longer A Lucky Cat.

While I was slowly dying, time passed and then I heard Human voices and big rumbles of something digging. And then there was a round light.

'Here's a Cat! Poor Puss! Lay still. We'll get you out. Careful... careful. Don't struggle.'

I was dug out and they carried me away. Soon Big Human came and took me to another place. I heard 'Hotel'. It was wonderful. Even being put in warm water all over again was wonderful. But I couldn't eat. It hurt.

My Adopted Humans took me to another Human who opened my mouth and looked inside. Then it felt all over my body and put something sharp in me. I went to sleep. When I woke up my butt was sore and my tail was very painful. This Human said, 'He's spayed now and his is tail will heal' and it put something wet on my tail and wrapped it up.

Back at the Hotel, Big Human said, 'This is an omen. We must celebrate. Lucifer! I have a special gift for you. Here is some caviar. Eat up.'

I sniffed. I licked. It was not good so I yawned.

I couldn't eat at all. I just wanted to rest and be stroked now and then. I slept a lot. But one day My Big Human was lying on my special sleeping place. It was reading the newspaper and something was smelling good. I jumped up to investigate. On its chest was a ham sandwich. I picked it up. I was polite about it. I took it behind the resting place and ate it.

And after that everything began to come right. We moved to a new place with softness to pad on and cosy sleeping places but at first, no Human smells. My appetite came back. I put on weight. My tail didn't grow but soon it was fat and fluffy. My Adopted Humans were very proud of me. All their friends admired me. They would say, 'How lucky you three have been!'

Three! I am included. I am loved I am, after all, A Lucky Cat.

THE STREET PHOTOGRAPHER

Summer 1933

The man with only one grey suit was preparing to leave for work. He had woken as usual at seven o'clock when the car dealership opposite his rented room opened the doors to its workshop with a bang and the Bottle-O opposite dropped a large quantity of bottles into one of its storage bins. He peered through the grimy window. Three young bottle-collecting boys in raggedy clothes, their hands in their pockets and only one wearing shoes, stood beside the truck until the boss, Stan, hopped out of the cab and doled out their earnings for their previous night's work – just a few pennies.

The man at the window, observing this exchange, remarked to himself 'Looks like a nice day.' Still wearing the old singlet he had worn to bed, he washed himself in the cracked basin in the mouldy little bathroom down the hall. He shaved and with his towel over his shoulder and patting his face dry, went back into his room to put the kettle on the gas hob.

'Hmm ... ' he confirmed to himself, taking another quick squiz out the grimy back window. 'Can probably risk the brown shoes today.' His brown shoes had a hole in each sole so he only wore them on fine days. The tops, however, were well-polished and still looked presentable and they were more comfortable than his black pair which, second hand, were newer although not yet completely broken in. Comfort was a priority as it was Friday and he would be working late.

He peered into the tannin-stained depths of the tin teapot. Quite a lot of tea leaves in there still looking useable. He added an economical half teaspoonful of fresh leaves and poured on the boiling water. He placed two slices of bread on a toasting fork and held them over the gas flame, turning them until they were nicely browned then ate them with a meagre spread of jam. Then, after dressing, choosing a tie from his selection of three, and a quick inspection in the bathroom mirror which only provided a reflection of the top half of him, he donned his brown trilby, patted his pockets to make sure he had enough business cards and his permit, picked up his camera and bag containing rolls of film and closing the door of the dreary little room, he set off down the stairs passing the dentist's surgery on the first floor. The door had a frosted glass window with "Dr Robert Pullen DDS – Dental Surgeon and Prosthodontist" in black and gold lettering and a poster declaring 'Specialising in false teeth' and the reassuring message 'With particular attention to comfort'. A framed illustration of a man and a woman with identical straight smiles adorned the wall to the right of the door.

At the street level the man in the grey suit turned right towards the harbour walking past the grocer, butcher, milk bar, fruiterer, tearooms and finally, on the corner opposite the wharf, the Masonic Hotel – known by the locals as "The Mosso" – Devonport's weekend day-tripper drawcard with its open-air garden overlooking the harbour. A few unemployed men were hanging around the side entrance to the Bar.

The 8 o'clock ferry was in the process of docking and soon the gangplank was shoved into place with only a dozen or so passengers disembarking, climbing up to the level of the wharf as the tide was low. The crowd of waiting passengers skidded down the gangplank – the few ladies who were boarding and wearing high heels clinging onto the railing. The funnel blew a triumphant farewell blast and they were off, the steam engine throbbing. Most went inside and sat on the slatted benches reading the morning newspapers but the man in the grey suit remained out on the deck. He would pick up a discarded copy as they disembarked. No point in spending an unnecessary penny ha'penny.

He sat at the stern, both arms stretched along the gunwale, the wake of the ferry foaming beneath him. What a bonza day! Blue sky, blue harbour, the sun already promising a warm day with just a gentle breeze. Devonport on the North Shore receded behind him, its little houses diminishing in their residential cluster along the shoreline and even the white Masonic Hotel with its dignified Victorian façade seemed to lose its prominence from a distance.

The Ferry Building tower clock chimed the half hour as the man in the grey suit disembarked and set off heading towards his allotted site on the corner of Vulcan Lane. He passed the jobless lines trailing along Quay Street and around the corner into an alley. Men in worn suits and hats, leaning on walls, mainly silent, dejectedly hopeful that this day they just might be amongst the chosen few to help unload the merchant ships. Every morning they came and every evening they went home to somewhere poor and wretched – a homeless shelter, a boarding house, even their own suburban houses and if the weather was fine, they bedded down right where they stood. 'Poor blighters' thought the man in the grey suit. He walked on.

Just as he was standing waiting to cross Customs Street he spotted the young woman. My, she was a corker! She was on the opposite side of the street and when the traffic cleared, she stepped confidently off the kerb and walked towards him with long purposeful strides. She was wearing a slim very feminine white dress and a knotted bandeau to match and as she approached he raised his camera and took several shots of her. She hadn't noticed him and looked startled when she reached the pavement on his side of the road and he handed her his card. She didn't acknowledge him but she took the card in her gloved hand without slowing her pace and walked briskly on. He watched her to see if she would discard the card but she didn't.

'Oy mate! Whadda ya think you're up to? This is my patch!' A spivvy joker in a striped blazer was accosting him just as he was walking past the GPO. He had a greasy looking waxed moustache to match his dyed black hair and a straw boater on at a jaunty angle. He shoved his Kodak in the offender's face, waving it back and forth. 'See this? Ey? Ey? ' he said aggressively. 'This is my stand. Let's see y'permit.'

'Sorry cobber – I'm Permit No.22 – with Hammond & Webster.' And the man in the grey suit hurried away up the main street.

***

Bid Briggs entered the Shell Oil Company foyer. It was a brand-new building – just grand with its impressive lobby in the art deco style and its row of lifts with their shiny brass doors. Little pings sounded as each lift reached the lobby and the doors automatically slid back.

An elevator girl in her smart uniform and white gloves pulled back the interior cage doors with a clatter and greeted each passenger with a 'Good Morning Sir. Good Morning Madam.' Bid always rather liked being elevated to a 'madam' even though she was only nineteen and a junior in the pecking order of the staff department.

Today was Friday and she was wearing her best outfit because after work on Fridays, which was late night shopping, she and some of her girlfriends would meet and walk up and down Queen Street looking in the shop windows and then go to Ann's Pantry to indulge in their delicious pies – a guilty extravagance in these hard times.

Bid, whose given name was Louise, knew how lucky she was to have a job. When the Great Depression struck, like all the employees at The Shell Oil Company, Bid was terrified that she'd lose her job, but the Company was remarkably fair when it became necessary to reduce staff. They investigated each employee's individual circumstances. Those who came from well off families who could support them were let go. Bid definitely didn't fit into that category, living at home with her mother and brother and the only one employed. True, her mother was a dressmaker but often her clients didn't pay and her brother, a motor mechanic, had been laid off and only earned a bit here and there doing backyard repairs.

In the Staff Room she placed her headband, gloves and handbag in her locker and headed towards the Typists' Room. In the hallway she passed Walter Laurence, one of the travellers. He smiled and raised his hat to her as they were passing and Bid's heart took a little leap. She had a crush on Walter. He was so handsome and so courteous and she wished so much he would ask her out but, as a traveller he was away a lot, driving around the North Island, visiting clients and making sure they kept their accounts with Shell and didn't get poached by competitors. Actually, Walter was quite famous throughout Shell New Zealand as he had entered Shell's worldwide competition to submit a new slogan for their forthcoming international advertising campaign. Walter had entered *Go Well, Go Shell* and it had won and was now to be seen on Shell billboards all around the world and the lyrics were used in an advertising jingle on the radio. Gosh! Fancy being that clever and handsome as well! Bid, true to her age, indulged in her fair share of dreaming but in fact she was a realist and the thought of Walter Laurence even noticing her was simply too blissful and impossible for words. Anyway, he was far too old for her – must be at least twenty-seven.

Bid opened the door of the typists' room. Known as The Typing Pool, she was assaulted by the thunderous sound of a myriad of clattering typewriters. She settled down at her desk. Already there were memos to be typed up, written in a variety of legible and illegible hands. As a junior Bid had been, until today, allotted all the easy tasks. But yesterday she had been elevated to a secretarial position and appointed to Mr. Stormont, a very nice man with a moustache and a permanent smile who was so awfully nice to Bid, addressing her as Miss Briggs. He was very considerate and didn't dictate too fast.

At 5 o'clock the closing bell sounded and all the girls in The Typing Pool immediately put the covers on their typewriters and headed out the door. Bid collected her belongings from her locker and went into the rest room to freshen up – renewing her lipstick, carefully putting the bandeau on and arranging her mid blond wavy hair in a flattering way to frame her face. Then she left the building and walked briskly back up the main street to meet her girlfriends on the corner of Vulcan Lane.

***

Despite the unsettling encounter with 'Boater Joker', Bill Benson – the man in the grey suit – had had a good day so far. He'd arrived at his allotted site around 9 o'clock to be greeted by Stuart Harvey whose stand was up on the corner of Albert Street.

'G'day Sport!' Stu was a cheery bloke, always up for a natter.

'Here's hoping it's a good day' he remarked, glancing around at the last of the office or shop workers hurrying by. 'Probably won't see much action 'til around 11 o'clock when the ladies arrive in town.'

Bill Benson nodded and the two chatted for a while until Stuart said, 'Well ... better be on m'way. No peace for the wicked' and set off up the street at a cracking pace.

Bill lit a cigarette. He was trying to limit himself to ten a day to cut down on costs. Every penny counted although things had been looking up since he'd been given the Vulcan Lane site. Lots of foot traffic there, right on the corner of Queen Street and some very swanky shops not only in the main street but up Vulcan Lane as well. Elwyn Shoes was up there – one of the best shoe stores in town. And John Court's Department store was only a few doors up the street. Every woman stopped at their windows to admire the beautiful array of hats, gowns and fabrics.

Bill threw down the match and noted the cuffs of his grey suit were starting to show signs of fraying. Not a good look! Not at all. But he couldn't even consider buying a new suit or even a second hand one – not just yet. Iris came first.

Since his new location he had been able to increase the money he sent her every week to £1. And he'd been able to afford the furnished room at Devonport. Dingy though it was it was better than that boarding house in Grey Lynn. Quieter too and he rather enjoyed taking the ferry to work even though that added a small cost to his weekly outgoings. No, he must make do for a little longer in the suit department. Make sure he captured lots of shots, especially as business was best in summer and early autumn.

And Iris, still living in Hamilton, said she was doing just fine renting the room at Mrs. Somers'. It was just a short walk across the river to her job in town where recently she'd been able to find work as a waitress. With the money Bill was sending plus her own wage she was managing to put a bit aside every week to deposit into their savings account, the plan being that once they had accrued enough money she would join Bill in Auckland and they'd be able to afford to rent a little flat.

Waitressing was a definite let down from Iris' previous job as a sales assistant at the furniture store Miller & Booth. That was where they had met, she and Bill. He had been the Company Accountant but when the Depression really cut into what had been a thriving business, Mr Miller and Mr Booth were forced to close down. So both Iris and Bill were out of work and as the Depression deepened and neither could find employment, Bill decided to go up to Auckland to try his luck there. A bloke he had recently encountered in the pub had mentioned that unemployed men had been doing alright there, taking photo snaps of people who were just walking along the street! He'd always been a keen photographer and possessed a nice Leica which fortunately he hadn't sold. He and

Iris had slowly sold all their possessions for pathetic returns so that now they had nothing left to sell apart from their essential clothing which included Bill's one remaining suit. He applied to Hammond and Webster and was appointed to a starter site up in Karangahape Road. He must have done alright up there to have been promoted to this prime spot.

By 11 o'clock business was hotting up. Ladies were arriving by tram for a visit to town. They were wearing their best summer dresses and hats and gloves along with their best shoes. They were mostly married women out for the day with a friend or a mother and some with very young children holding their hands. Bill got some smashing shots and was pleased to notice that nearly every lady kept the card he handed to them. Hopefully they'd return another day to go to the Hammond & Webster booth to look at the prototypes and order quantities of his photographs.

Street photography was growing into quite a big business since The Depression when traditional photographers suffered a serious downturn in their studio business and reinvented themselves. Licensing laws were eventually introduced and the photographic companies secured specific territories in which their team of street photographers could legally operate.

Business was easing off by mid-afternoon. Bill had used up quite a few rolls of film and was optimistic about the potential of the day but, despite the advantage of the more comfortable brown shoes, his feet were tired and his legs were aching. He took a break, leaning against a wall around the corner in the lane and had just lit a cigarette when he was accosted by a man in a smart suit and a trilby saying 'Benson?' and upon Bill's acknowledgement the man said sharply

'Mr. Hammond wants to see you – quick smart' and he set off up Vulcan Lane walking very fast towards the Company's office in High Street, leaving Bill no option but to follow.

Mr. Hammond had a very long narrow face, a matching chin, thin lips and a cap of shiny slicked down dark hair. He wore a pair of small round spectacles with dark rims which gave him the appearance of a very stern schoolmaster or, at worst, a Dickensian undertaker. He remained seated when Bill entered his office and didn't invite him to sit down. He was obviously very displeased.

'I've had a complaint from Taylor & Fresco.' Mr. Hammond went straight into full attack mode.

'Yes' he continued. 'I understand you were taking photographs down near the Quay this morning. Taylor & Fresco's man has submitted an objection'. He stared intently at Bill who remained silent.

'You know this is totally out of line Benson and is a case for dismissal. The agreements between street photography companies have to be abided by otherwise we would have *mayhem.*' Mr. Hammond nodded in confirmation of this dramatic statement and his eyebrows shot up above his glasses with astonishing speed. Bill could see he was now waiting for him to speak so he said –

'Well Mr. Hammond, Sir – I admit I … well I did take a photograph that's true. But just one. A lady. I truly didn't think. She was walking towards me and … ' He petered out at that point. Any further attempt at an excuse seemed fruitless.

Mr. Hammond stared at Bill for what seemed like minutes. He was weighing up his options. Here he had a good earner and Benson seemed a quality sort of person – well spoken, well-groomed although his suit had seen better days. But he was the style of man who would appeal to the ladies. Not threatening. He had a gentlemanly air about him and was the sort of person that Hammond & Webster liked to employ. And Taylor & Fresco's Permit No.9 down near the Quay – well he'd caught a glimpse of that chap one day when he was going to the GPO. Most unsuitable. A rakish oily sort of fellow. Not at all the kind of man he'd like to see representing his business. Mind you, that stand's location was a winner, capturing all the foot traffic to and from the ferry buildings *and* the train, tram and bus terminals. Yes – wouldn't he like to get his hands on *that* location. He returned his thoughts to the present. He'd let Benson stand there and squirm for a minute or two longer.

Bill waited. He'd interviewed job applicants during his time as Accountant at Miller & Booth and sensed it was best to keep his mouth shut and let the Boss enjoy playing his little game of having the upper hand. The ploy worked. Mr. Hammond finally adjusted his glasses, tapped his fingers on his blotter and said, 'The photograph, or photographs you took of the lady ... the film must be given to Taylor & Fresco. You can leave it with us and we'll take care of it. But this is your one and only warning mind! We can't have bad blood between competitors. We're dealing with enough complications at present with complaints from the City Council who are targeting us and issuing fines because of the increasing quantity of littering!' Mr. Hammond's eyebrows shot up again with startling alacrity. They almost looked as if they would detach themselves from his forehead and shoot up and hit the ceiling. 'No – we don't need the additional problem of friction between competitors' he added, giving Bill the stare once again.

And Bill responded 'Of course Mr. Hammond, Sir. It won't happen again I assure you. Thank you Sir and I apologise for causing this unintended complication.'

'Yes, yes.' Mr. Hammond waved his long thin fingers in a dismissive way as if Bill was some recalcitrant schoolboy.

Bill left the office and walked down into the street. The feeling of relief was so huge that he decided he'd pop into the little teashop in the lane and treat himself to a piece of cake and a cuppa. A bit of chocolate would pep him up ready for the influx of business when the office girls finished work and started their Friday night parading up and down Queen Street. Good business coming up!

***

Bid and her friends met at their prearranged time on the corner of Vulcan Lane. They stood chatting and giggling and occasionally looking about them at the passers-by in case some nice young men might come strolling along. Then they linked arms and started to walk up the pavement towards John Court's. Bill at that moment spotted them and dashed in front of them walking backwards to take the photo. They all smiled, stopped walking and posed for him (what a humdinger!) and at that moment Bill realised that the young woman in white that he had photographed that morning was one of the group. She didn't appear to recognise him as Bill handed out cards to them all. They resumed their stroll up the street laughing and talking.

Bill moved to the side of the pavement to stand out of the way of the crowd while he removed the film from his camera to replace it with a new one and just as he did he was hit on the side of this head with a brain shattering blow. He dropped the used film and the assailant quickly scooped it up and ran off up Vulcan Lane. Bill, staggering and holding his head, just had time to glimpse the striped jacket, the slick back of the bounder's head and the straw boater in his hand. Boater Joker! There was no doubt about it! No point in trying to catch him. Couldn't afford to miss out on the best earning day of the week. No … he'd keep working and decide what to do about it later. That slimy character had overplayed his hand but he was too stupid to know it.

***

Back in his room that evening, Bill sat down to write two letters.

In the first, in his refined Accountant's hand, he wrote:

Dear Mr. Hammond,

I wish to apologise profusely Sir for my error of judgement this morning and to thank you for your generous decision to allow me to retain my representation with your esteemed organisation. Confiscating the film and transferring it to Taylor & Fresco's ownership was the only fair and ethical action to take under the circumstances.

However, Mr. Hammond, may I respectfully enquire as to whether you have already passed the film to the other party as I have a very grave incident to report which may change your mind. This evening, Friday the 20th of February at approximately five minutes to six, I was attacked by Taylor & Fresco's licensee who works Stand No. 9 outside the General Post Office. This ruffian punched me severely on the side of my head and while I was incapacitated, stole the completed film which I was removing from my camera. He then ran off and as I was in no condition to pursue him, I made a business decision to remain on my stand and continue my evening's work. I have several witness statements written by members of the public who observed the attack and subsequent theft and these I enclose with this letter.

Of course, Sir, it will be entirely your decision as to whether you decide it is appropriate to act in some way, if at all, with regard to this outrage and I leave it in your capable hands with complete confidence.

I am sure you will wish to be assured that I am in good health with just a slight headache because of some minor swelling to the side of my head and that I shall be continuing to man my site according to the Company's established schedules.

I am, Sir,

Your loyal representative,

William H. Benson, Permit No.22'

Bill reread the letter several times and after making a couple of amendments, sealed it in an envelope. He then wrote to Iris.

'My Darling Dear Girl,

Just a few lines to let you know that all is going swimmingly here. Business gets better every day and I am really enjoying my new stand. It's in a topping location – one of the best and the firm are treating me very well indeed and always on the minute with their commissions. And my cosy new room in Devonport is just the ticket.

Precious one, I strongly believe it will only be a short time before we can be together again and meantime don't worry about me one little bit. I'm feeling in the pink. I just hope you are as well and not finding the work too taxing.

I send you a thousand kisses and hugs,

You devoted husband,

Bill

He sealed the letter and wrote the address adding a drawing of a heart on the bottom left-hand corner of the envelope with an arrow through it pointing to his wife's name 'Mrs. William Benson'.

***

Summer 1942

Enjoying the warm sunny morning Bill Benson walked through Albert Park on his way to the office. He felt happy and contented as he ambled along the avenue under the great oaks and between flower beds filled with hectically coloured marigolds and red salvia. 'Never been keen on municipal planting.' he ruminated. 'All that red and yellow.'

And then his thoughts turned back to all that had happened over the past nine years. What a contrast his life was now. How fortunate it had been that he had taken a punt during that brief encounter in Hamilton and, on the basis of an unlikely tip, headed for Auckland to try to earn some sort of a living by taking photographic snaps of unsuspecting people who were merely walking along a street. Leaving Iris behind had been awful but they had both agreed that they could think of no other alternative at the time. They could never have predicted that standing on a corner in all weathers with a camera as his tool of trade could have led to his current elevated occupation and the ability to buy their own cosy little house in Parnell. And now, even better, they were the proud parents of two lovely little daughters.

He entered Hammond & Webster's offices which occupied the first floor at 127 High Street. The door of his office bore the name "Mr. William H. Benson – Company Accountant". Bill had been appointed to this position in 1938 when the previous Accountant had retired. Iris had joined him in Auckland a few years before. They had rented an old cottage in Devonport and Iris, by a stroke of luck, had landed a bookkeeping job with a local business. Street photography was booming so gradually they had built up a nice little nest egg in an interest-bearing savings account.

***

After the Boater Joker incident back in 1933, Mr. Hammond had kept an eye on Bill Benson. He had acted promptly on Bill's letter and reported the attack to the police. Licensee No.9 received a hefty sentence and was still residing in Mt Eden gaol having been convicted of Robbery with Assault and Battery. Bill continued to work his site down on the corner of Vulcan Lane and became Hammond & Webster's top earner. Mr. Hammond would occasionally take the short walk down to Bill's stand, watching him engage with shoppers, most of whom responded to him positively. His standard of photography was consistent, he was extremely reliable and the volume of sales of his photographs were profuse. Mr. Hammond delved into Bill's employment history and discovered that he was a qualified Accountant. He took a mental note of that. Should there be any administrative changes in the Company in future, William H. Benson could be just their man.

Shortly after his promotion Bill investigated the current trading position of Taylor & Fresco and, by gleaning information via industry gossip, discovered that they were under some financial strain so he approached Mr. Hammond with the suggestion that they make a very conservative offer to buy them out. This acquisition substantially increased the number of stands under the Hammond & Webster banner including the desirable GPO site and made them the dominant photographic company in Auckland because Bill also started to work on reinstating studio photography. Despite the Depression people continued to get engaged, married, commission professional portraits for business purposes and there was a huge demand when enlistment commenced at the start of the Second World War with families commissioning portraits of their sons in uniform before their assignment overseas. A state-of-the-art photographic studio now occupied the entire ground floor of 127 High Street.

***

Bill and Bid's paths crossed serendipitously one more time. As Company Accountant, Bill continued to take an interest in the street photography department and one day while he was in the developing studio he was captured by a particularly enchanting photo of two women and a child walking in Queen Street. The grandmother was elegantly dressed, slim and very stylish. The child, holding onto her gloved hand and that of a young woman, presumably her mother, was a tiny fairylike creature, probably three years' old with pale blond curls and wearing an exquisitely embroidered dress. And the young mother, smiling down at her daughter? Well, she was still a smasher in a pretty floral dress and flattering hat. Bill recognised her immediately. She was the young lady in the white dress – the one Bill had impulsively snapped in that contentious street photo way back in '33. She would never know that she had been a catalyst – an influential accident in the fortunes of an anonymous street photographer's life. And she, in turn, had taken her own path in ways that Bill Benson would never know.

He looked up the name on the order form. 'Mrs. Walter Laurence'.

FLIGHTS OF THE MIND

*Thoughts are like butterflies * catch them, hold them * for they are fleeting * like vaporised dreams * that float away*

There! She was into the book at last. She had harnessed her wandering mind enough to connect with the two main characters and at last she'd arrived at Chapter Two. Convinced she was focused at last she'd read on.

Rowena turned her head to stare out the window. A glossy black crow flashed across the view like a sinister jet plane on a bombing raid. She was acquainted with this crow because, apart from its strutting ownership of her back lawn, she had encountered it sitting on a branch midway down the cypress hedge. The twig in its beak was obviously longer than it would wish as it was trying to split it on a branch. This achieved it flew up into the heavy canopy where Ro could see a dense brown thicket high up in the furry green of the hedge and guessed that it was a nest. Crows! She hated them. Well – that was an exaggeration. How often, she mused, do we say we hate something when it is just an intense dislike. "Hate" is an extreme and dangerous feeling and lately she found herself using the word far too loosely.

Ro's mind took a sharp detour, typical during these days of recovery, to think about a TV personality she had viewed recently who, relating the subject of a particularly violent and horrifying crime, used the word "animal" to describe the perpetrator. Ro was incensed by this insult and had even tweeted said commentator politely imploring that he refrain from using a simile such as this. She was convinced, deep within her heart, that animals, plants and human infants were the only innocent beings on the planet.

This profound thought slid off the screen in a trice and skidded onwards. Yes... she watched far too much television. She constantly berated herself over this and yet she continued to feed the habit. Recovering from the illness there had been some excuse but she was better now. TV was addictive. Relaxing – sitting there in her favourite chair she would slouch into it, burrow down into it, curl up in it, plump and cuddle its cushions to warm up all the cold bits of her. Mindless! There seemed no need to exercise the mind when it just cruised along with the vision and the voices. And then would come the disconnection with the narrative and she'd wake up from a little snooze, the head lolling, the neck in agony, dozy, slumping – the mind becoming lazier and lazier, its alacrity eroding minute by minute.

Exasperated, Ro thrust herself out of the chair and walked out into the garden. It was the bluest of spring days – still and perfectly implicitly warm. She looked up at the fresh leaves on the great pin oak. They were barely moving so gentle was the breeze. She craned her neck to view the top of the tree. The soaring branches were rocking imperceptibly but above them, so far above them, sailing purposefully forward at a steady pace was a long dense white cloud. A free spirit in that empty blueness it thrust onwards as if it was on a mission. The front was pointed like the prow of a ship then it bellied out into a mass of cotton wool. Riding alongside it were its chicks – fat white puffs of spun sugar – gambolling – keeping up – racing forward. The mass was moving at such speed that it took less than thirty seconds to pass over the garden and head out towards the ocean.

She imagined she was in a plane. That cloud was moving as fast and as high as a jetliner so she would be there, gazing out, sailing along beside it. She thought of other clouds she had seen in her travels. In a plane, rocking and swaying blind in a grubby grey soup of suffocating wooliness with a feeling of dread in case the instrument landing system failed and then the feeling of relief as the plane descended and emerged gradually from the gloom. Or passing horizontal streaking clouds resting motionless in front of vivid white alps with a jade green fiord below. Or as a guest in the cockpit for that memorable landing in the sunset, cutting through streaks of wispy tulle, the welcoming lights of the immense port twinkling below through a pink haze. Then fear on a journey as the plane bounced and dropped through a tropical storm. Towering pillars of cumulous, their interiors illuminated with flashes of red, orange and white lightning, appeared to be putting on a performance for the audience inside that speeding metal tube.

And then the ultimate fear as she had boarded the aircraft out of that great city, the day she found the lump. Staying in the glossy hotel on the waterfront she had woken and started preparing for her day of meetings. Showering she had found it – the lump. She dressed and in denial set off on the business of the day but by lunchtime fear was inserting itself and by mid-afternoon she was on her way to the airport to take the first available flight home.

Ro looked towards the East. The cloud was travelling on, far in the distance now. Like her thoughts. Like the fear.

ROAD TRIP

The Canadian Police Officer was walking towards us. He was a heavy bloke with a stern expression beneath his Mounties hat. Jenny wound down the window of the pale metallic blue Cadillac.

'Hi Officerrr! Oh my God – was I speeding? Oh shucks, not again. Honestly Officerrr, I was so excited to be showing my friends the scenery that I didn't realise...'

She waved her arm in an introductory gesture.

'Now, this is my friend Lucy here in the passenger seat. She's from Australia and this is her Mom who's come all the way from New Zealand. Imagine that? This is her very first trip to The Rockies.'

She giggled. Jenny giggled after making almost every statement. Actually, it was rather more of a cackle than a giggle. She gave the Officer a welcoming smile.

Implacable, the Police Officer stared back at her.

'Licence please.' He was unmoved. 'Where are you off to?' he asked, scanning the licence.

'Oh everywhere Officerrr.' Giggling.

'Next stop Lake Louise but we're going everywhere, y'know, Banff, Jasper – all over. We've come from Vancouver Island. That's where I live.' Jenny nodded confidentially. 'Near Duncan. Cute little town. D'you know it?'

The Officer cut her off.

'Well Ma'am – you're getting short of points here.' He stabbed the licence with his forefinger.

'Oh My God – I *know*. How many have I got left?' Chummy chuckling.

'Two Ma'am. It's not looking good for you.' He handed back the licence.

'I'm goin' to give you a pass this time' he continued, glancing at my mother and me sternly as if he was doing us the favour.

'You'd better concentrate more or it's likely you'll all be taking your friends on public transport – back to that little place of yours.'

'Oh Officerrr. That is so kind of you…

But the Officer was strolling back towards his shiny vehicle, his broad back showing his lack of interest. He slowly squeezed himself in, turned off the flashing lights and drove off.

'Oh My God! How about that?' Jenny swung out onto the road. 'I'd better watch my speed otherwise you'll be driving.'

Cackling she elbowed me.

***

We arrived at Lake Louise mid-afternoon. Canada was experiencing a late Spring and the lake was still frozen solid. The scene lived up to the travel brochures. It was utterly beautiful. Jenny swept into the foyer and up to Reception, proffering an executive business card to the clerk who appeared to be impressed. Jenny never revealed who the influential friend was that the card belonged to. Mum and I, following her like a pair of obedient puppies, hovered around in the background. My mother was speechless, still recovering from the encounter with the Police Officer. She'd met Jenny years ago when she was just a perky twenty-year-old, touring the world solo but this was Mum's first experience of the wealthy, married Jenny in full hostess mode.

There was a three-bedroom suite booked for us. Jenny swept around the entire apartment, looking behind sofas, pulling back bedcovers as if she was inspecting a crime scene.

Ha! Behind a toilet she found a cigarette butt. She was on the phone immediately demanding to see the Assistant Manager. He came promptly and she pointed out the offending butt, demanding an upgrade.

I went into my mother's room to find she had unzipped her bag. She was proactively settling in as she was already holding an unpacked piece of clothing in her hand.

'We're moving' I announced.

'What? Why?' Mum was bewildered. She'd never before stayed in such luxury but she obediently zipped up her bag, picked up her handbag and trotted along behind Jenny and me. We ended up in one of the chateaux's towers in an even more glamorous suite, which, fortunately passed Jenny's rigorous inspection.

***

In Banff, rather than staying at the famous hotel, Jenny had decided we should stay in our own cabin. It was cosy and welcoming with an open log fire to toast us and a fridge full of delicious food. Next morning, when we woke, it was snowing. Deer were roaming around near the cabin which was utterly magical to my mother.

***

We left Banff, after a couple of days – destination Jasper – setting off at Jenny's usual driving speed – fast. She just couldn't help herself. And so, inevitably, along the way an oncoming patrol car turned on its flashing lights and executing a deft U-turn, pulled up in front of us.

'Oh my God! Not again!' Jenny was outraged.

This officer was slowly unfolding himself from his vehicle. He was slim and tall. He stood beside his driver's door for a moment adjusting his Sam Browne, checking his general appearance and after placing his hat perfectly on his head, advanced toward us in his long leather boots. He was absolutely gorgeous and he knew it. He slowly approached Jenny's window and as she gave him one of her most endearing smiles, he responded displaying a set of teeth that complimented his outfit.

'Oh Officerrr! I'm *so* sorry. Was I speeding?' Guilty giggling.

'Well yes Ma'am, you were.' Still smiling he leant his elbow on the open driver's window sill in a relaxed and friendly way.

'I'm sorry too. I'll have to ask you for your licence.

'Of course!' Jenny handed it over and launched into a litany of our travels so far, punctuated with numerous Jenny giggles.

'Well that sounds just fine Ma'am. Are you enjoying yourselves?'

He directed this charming enquiry to my mother and me. We nodded away, muttering about what a great time we were having, when Jenny launched into…

'Yes Officerrr. We've come all the way up from Vancouver Island. I live near Duncan. On the lake. Do you know it?

'Well yes Ma'am, it just so happens I do. I've got relatives who live quite near there. It's a beautiful place. Well now. You *have* travelled quite a distance. Where are you off to next?'

'Jasper' Jenny replied, bestowing him with another of her most engaging smiles.

'Oh boy, it's gorgeous Ma'am. I know it well. Now there's a great little place to eat there that I really recommend. I'll give you the details.'

He dug around in his jacket pockets and produced a card. 'There y'go. Enjoy.'

'We will' Jenny responded. 'Thanks so much Officerrr.'

Dream Boy raised a thumb and distributed another blinding smile.

'Just hold tight' he said and sauntered off to his cruiser.

He returned with a traffic ticket and presented it to Jenny as if he was giving her a rose.

'Now you all enjoy yourselves.' He was smiling at Mum and me. Stepping back he gave us a salute then, giving Jenny the eye he said, 'Now mind how you go. You've only got one point left on your speeding record. Have a nice day.'

He saluted again, returned to his vehicle and drove away.

***

At Jasper we stayed right on the lake. The thaw had begun and it looked like a crystalline pale green sorbet. Ducks alighted on the surface and fluttering their wings and waggling their tails, created little jade green swimming pools which grew bigger and bigger as they swam around.

By this time I was driving the Cadillac. We drove into town to visit the café the officer had recommended. After the shock of receiving the ticket, Jenny had rather gone off him but we persuaded her to give it a try. We hopped out of the Caddy and returning to it after an excellent meal, discovered I had locked the keys inside the car. While we were having a debate about where to find someone lurking around who was an experienced car thief, Judy suddenly yelled, 'Hey! I seem to remember Frank telling me at some stage about taping a spare key to the exhaust.'

Down I went onto the bitumen, lying on my back, feeling around along the tube which was caked with dry congealed mud. I found a bump and scratching away, breaking a few finger nails in the process, there indeed was a key.

Boy did I fall in love with Frank at that very moment and as a reward I wrote him a poem. It was titled 'How Frank did something right for a change and saved the day.' It lived for many years, beautifully framed, on the wall of Frank's Bar at Grove Hall, their estate at Duncan.

***

My mother and I did a lot of overseas travelling together after my father's death and in the diary she kept about this particular trip, she pronounced it the one in which she had had the most giggles.

THE ANNUAL ESSAY COMPETITION

At morning Assembly we are all packed into the school hall. I loathe crowds and usually manage to stand on the end of the line but today I am squeezed in the middle beside my best friend Bridgette who does tend to be a bit over-emotional at times. Today she is a total mess. She's sobbing loudly which eventually leads to a black robed Mrs Chautelle, affectionately known as 'Chortle', appearing at the end of the row and beckoning me – I'm considered 'A Responsible Girl' – to 'bring that girl out.'

I grab Bridge's hand and drag her through the crush. 'Chortle', a quick decision maker, says, 'She'd better go home.'

Bearing the burden of my reputation I have to make a decision, so I tow Bridge along The Covered Way, through the school gardens to the main gates to wait for a tram – Bridge snivelling into her soggy hankie. I give her mine. She boards the tram and, standing on the back platform, sails off along the lines sobbing – 'The King's dead!'

I wave limply until the tram rounds a corner and then hurry to my classroom.

It's the 6th of February 1952 and whilst I am sad about the King, today is a big day – The Annual Essay Competition. I won it last year, so it's difficult not to feel competitive.

Our English mistress, Miss Christobel Ash, enters the classroom. She's small and timid, her slight body overwhelmed by her black gown. Our class gives her a hard time now and then, but we're actually rather fond of her.

'Gels!' – her voice is just a little more forceful than a whisper. 'Your instructions providing this year's selection of titles are on your desks. You have ninety minutes.'

She taps the button on the little silver bell on her desk, presses her stopwatch and says, 'Start now.'

There's silence in the classroom while everyone chews their pencils and then, almost in unison, dip our heads over our papers. As we begin to write the silence is overtaken by scribbly noises on generations of graffiti-carved desktops.

Despite numerous stern warnings from the parents about the evils of being prideful, I can't help feeling the pressure of being last year's winner. It makes me think so hard my brain hurts. I study the list.

'Making the best of things.'
'My favourite pastime'
'Windows'
'Ambition'
'The happiest day of my life'

I choose one and set off writing at a frustratingly slow pace.

WINDOWS by Lucy Laurence

A new house has been built next to ours. It's down in the gully hidden by a wild area at the bottom of our garden which we call 'The Tiger Country'. Dad gave this area its name because it's a perfect haven for the neighbourhood cats, being crowded with soaring bamboo and long grasses. We often play down there. It's a perfect setting for imaginative games.

One day, during a game based on our interpretation of The Delhi Durba inspired by a recent short at the local pictures about the Partitioning of India and wearing Mum's discarded floral dresses wound around our heads to represent turbans, we parted the bamboo so we could take a peek at the new house. The sparkling window confronting us was very clean and shiny and was dressed with a thick lace curtain.

Nothing much to see here we decided but, just as we began to close our bamboo curtain, the lace twitched then parted and we were confronted by a lady with a rather anxious and surprised expression. We bolted.

Shortly after a report to The Parents, our mother, who is a very kind and neighbourly person, took the trouble to whip up a batch of scones and pay a visit to the owner of the face. Her name is Mrs Booth and in no time my mother is calling her Sybil, reporting to us that she is a very nice woman who is a widow and has now settled in famously and is no longer anxious.'

I chew my pencil. 'Rake up another window' I instruct myself. 'Something familiar.'

My grandmother lives in a very old house and generally keeps her windows pretty clean. But if I go out onto her back verandah, turn right and walk to the end, there is the laundry known as the washhouse. And this window is nothing to be proud of. To be honest, it's positively opaque! When I stand on a stool to peer through it, the iron roof on the woodshed below looks a milky grey when it's actually red. This is because of all the ancient uninhabited spiders' webs that have formed a film all over the glass. On the sill there are grimy jars containing used paint brushes in rusty water; the remains of numerous ancient blocks of rock-hard yellow soap and used blue bags. This window definitely demeans Gran's housekeeping skills.'

More pencil chewing. I've picked the wrong title – that's for sure. Ah yes! I know... Down goes my head as my pencil navigates the bumpy surface of my desk. I begin...

'At the beach the windows never get cleaned. As Mum says 'It's a lost cause'. That's because of the salt spray.

Our beach house is pretty wonky to be frank but is located right on the beach. Well almost, as the sand has built up into a low bump graded by the tide. On it, beach grasses grow with furry flowers. We gather them. We dip the heads into water-colour solutions, placing them in jars on windowsills.

*And who cares about salt spray on these windows because we never look **at** them. We look **through** them. We fling them open. And how beautiful it is.*

Headlands jut out on either side to protect our bay. At low tide, the rocks are revealed decorated with oysters. In sandy patches cockles are hiding, betrayed by their clusters of bubbles. In rock pools tiny sea creatures scurry and swim, living their salty lives. Pohutukawa trees cling to the side of the cliffs – in summer ablaze with brushy red blooms.

The water in the bay never looks the same. Some days its blue and calm. Others it's jade green and oily. When the storms come it is grey with frothy white tops and the waves hurl foam onto the smooth wet sand.

Whatever its mood it is utterly beautiful.'

How's the time going? Another half hour? Time for one more window...

This window is different. It's a porthole and there is a row of them. They are on Mr Standish's yacht. He and Dad are great friends and sometimes our family is invited for a Sunday sailing day.

I press my nose to the round glass and the salty water glides past just below its base. When the craft lists the water rises and sometimes, on really wild days, the starboard gunwale is immersed and my little porthole displays a world of water – a mixture of blue and green. It's secretive and fascinating and busy with all manner of sea creatures on their own particular business.

*One day a pod of dolphins discovers our boat – diving, surfacing, rolling, flipping their shiny bodies. I watch them as they play – so close I could touch them. It is as if they are showing off – full of joy – laughing **with** me. I feel...*

The bell sounds!
'Pencils down.' Miss Ash's voice is bordering on forceful.

***

The mother in this story – my mother – kept letters and notebooks full of accounts of the past. I found this uncompleted essay amongst them – forgotten long ago. Thousands of days have passed – so many that that King's daughter has also died – and yet, suddenly I remembered that teenage episode so vividly. Why? Because, in retrospect, it was very funny,.

In 1952 I obviously didn't win the Annual Essay Competition but, in retrospect, who cares. It's 2025 and we are still going strong – Bridge and I.

In this challenging new world, a true lifelong friendship frosted with humour, is priceless.

THE DREAM

Lucy had had that horrible dream last night. The one in which she was in Coronation Road, her great grandfather's street, under its canopy of trees. She was walking along the pavement and came to a hole which some workmen must have dug because it was very neat and rectangular. In the hole, lying curled up on her side, there was a little girl, Lucy's age, no more than four years' old – crying.

That was the dream. Nothing further happened as Lucy always woke up at that moment. It was a repetitive dream and always left her feeling extremely disturbed and sad as the child's plight was never resolved and she had no idea who she was and the dream dissolved before she was able to help her.

Lucy was thinking about the dream as they chugged their way to the cemetery on a sunny Sunday in the winter of 1943. Great Aunt Flo was driving the big shiny black Morris. It had wide running boards and very slippery brown ribbed leather seats so that Lucy, sitting in the back, slid sideways and bumped into Gran when they turned a corner. Not that they ever went very fast. The pace was sedate and when Great Aunt Flo changed gears they wheezed.

They entered the cemetery gates driving through a beautiful avenue of native trees, past the tea house and the little chapel and along a narrow winding road until the graveyards came into view. Ancient headstones stood in rows along neatly mown grass paths, shaded in places by old trees. The family grave had a simple grey marble tombstone with lots of names in gold. It was surrounded by white marble pebbles with plaques set amongst them with more names on them. There seemed to be quite a lot of people packed into that small space.

Great Aunt Flo, Gran and Lucy's mother Louise, did a bit of tidying up – pulling up the odd weed or two that had grown amongst the marble pebbles, filling the vases at a tap nearby and replacing the dead flowers with fresh ones. Then they all got into the Morris again and drove down to St Heliers Bay where they sat on a seat to admire the view of the harbour. Rangitoto Island floated benignly in front of them.

'Well – time to go' said Great Aunt Flo, heaving herself to her feet with a great deal of huffing and puffing. She was wearing her usual black coat and hat and Lucy couldn't help looking at the hairs sprouting out of her chin. They piled into the Morris and proceeded at a stately pace along the waterfront road.

Around the little bays with houses sweeping up the hillsides and clinging to the cliffs. Past the shops and the park with the fountain that lit up at night. Past the yacht club and the boatyard where the big yachts were put up in winter to have their bottoms cleaned. Boys in small sailing boats sprinted around on the sparkling water participating in races, wheeling around marker buoys and setting their spinnakers. Busy ferries pottered back and forth to and from the North Shore.

It was a long drive up to Great Grandad's house where they would have afternoon tea. He would be sitting in his usual chair in the bay window, reading. Lucy liked to get behind his chair with its high winged back and tickle his bald head. He never disappointed. He would swipe his head and say 'Drat that fly!' over and over again, never spoiling the game.

It was always the same routine most Sundays when it was fine and was the only outing of the week for 'The War' was on somewhere else in the world and it was a quiet and uneventful time for the adults waiting at home in the Antipodes – living with much fear and anxiety.

***

It is 2017. Lucy is watching a documentary by Simon Schama, 'The History of the Jews'. A World War II scene appears of a street in Germany. In the grainy black and white film people are walking back and forth in front of shops, some with shattered windows and vile painted signs. On the pavement, alone, lies the little girl in Lucy's childhood dream.

Dead? The people walk past...

FAMILY MATTERS

It was starting to get dark. There were no people around, not even a dog to be seen out on an evening walk. Not that there was much of interest for dogs to sniff at or explore. It was just a vast estate of new houses – some completed, some already occupied with lights turned on and some half built with no roofs. Neat stacks of timber and corrugated iron lay around on the orange clay building sites. Roads with kerbing and pale concrete pavements wound around the estate but there was not a tree or foliage of any description to be seen. The emptiness made the sky look huge.

Lucy Laurence sat down on her small brown leather suitcase and had a good think. What was she to do? Where was she to go? She'd left home you see. She was running away. She was making a statement. She'd let them know she was serious by making a big thing of packing her suitcase, banging drawers and her wardrobe door to make sure they'd notice. Yes ... they needed to know she was serious.

At one point Mummy had come and stood leaning against the bedroom door jamb, her arms folded, saying 'Don't forget your toothbrush' in a matter-of-fact sort of way which was very offensive and which made Lucy stomp defiantly off to the bathroom. She couldn't believe it when she had finished her packing, had put on her gabardine coat and school hat which she hated but which was the only one she possessed and had stood on the mat in the front hall. Mummy came out of the kitchen with Nella on her hip and said,

'Well goodbye dear – you take care' and opened the front door. *She actually opened the front door for her!* And Lucy, unable to lose face, simply walked out. Daddy hadn't even got up out of his armchair to see her off! He stayed in the sitting room reading the newspaper and puffing away on his pipe.

So now she'd done it. What *was* she to do? She'd expected they would talk her out of it. Persuade her to stay. Plead with her. But they didn't. Surely they'd call out once she was a little way along the pavement and say, 'Come back Lucy! We're sorry!' But they didn't.

And now she was around the corner and they couldn't even see her! They didn't love her. They didn't care. She hated them all and that stupid baby sister. Oh yes ... they loved Nella alright but they didn't love her – Lucy. They couldn't possibly love her if they didn't even think about the fact that she was only seven years' old and she could be walking into DANGER! Oh, how could they *do* this to her?

The final rotten thing, the absolute last straw happened when she lost her temper with Nella. She was nothing but a nuisance. The *absolute pits* was when she ripped up and chewed – *chewed!* – Lucy's scrapbook with all the newspaper photos of the Royal Family in it – the princesses and everything. Lucy flew into a rage and was so upset that she slapped Nella on the face and her cheek became very red and of course she was bawling her eyes out and getting all the sympathy. And of course they thought it was all Lucy's fault. It just wasn't FAIR!

Lucy continued sitting on her suitcase and looked around. She really hated this place they were living in – *hated* it. So did Mummy, but Daddy had really had no choice. In 1946, when he came home from The War, Mummy, Nella and Lucy had to leave Grandma's house where they had been living while Daddy was away and return to this place where his job was. He went ahead of them in search of a house and he said they were jolly lucky to find this one as there was such a housing shortage. The Government had started building heaps of houses for this reason which Mummy and Daddy said was very good of them. But it was *awful*! Mind you, the house was okay because it was brand new and had that lovely smell of new wood and it had very pretty flowery wallpaper – a different design in every room.

But outside it was, as Mummy put it, 'A Sea of Clay'. There was a concrete path leading from the front door to the concrete path along the street and behind the house was a huge drain also made of concrete – very deep and wide with rushing water – so Lucy and Nella couldn't go outside and play in their own garden which hadn't happened anyway – yet.

There were no shops so Mummy had to squeeze herself into the one and only daily bus with all the other mothers to go and buy their food and Dad took the very early bus to work because they didn't have a car even though he worked for the Ford Motor Company for heaven's sake!

School was terrible. Too many rough kids and she particularly dreaded one subject – Composition. This was because she was really frightened of the teacher, Mr. Slevin, an angry old man who hadn't been to The War but who would have been absolutely perfect for killing Germans because he strode around the classroom swinging a leather strap. He never used it on the girls, just the poor little boys, but he would bang it loudly on the girls' desks just to keep them on their toes. So Lucy dreaded Composition even though she was actually quite good at English and writing stories. She started to develop a sore throat and would ask to go to the sick bay and eventually this was happening so often that the Headmistress called Mummy in and told her that she suspected Lucy was 'making it up'.

As a result of this something terrible happened. It was the most terrible thing that had happened to Lucy in her entire life ... so far.

Where Daddy was concerned telling lies was The Biggest Sin of All and so once Mummy reported Lucy's sin to him he was absolutely furious. His eyes became sort of very cold and next morning he made Lucy stand in front of him before he left for work. He told her this was a very grave thing she had done, to tell lies, and that he was very disappointed in her. He said that when he came home that evening she would be punished and so Lucy had to go to school with this feeling of dread about what might be going to happen. She definitely had a sore throat that day – all day.

As soon as Daddy got home he took Lucy into her bedroom and spanked her. She had never been so humiliated. She adored her father and she had thought he loved her because after he returned from The War, instead of calling her his pet name of Mrs McGurkinshaw, he started to call her Lae Lae which meant 'my love' on one of the islands in the Pacific Ocean apparently. And now here he was disapproving of her and even calling her Lucinda which proved how extremely serious it was. And the most awful thing was, she hadn't been telling lies. Her throat did hurt in Mr. Slevin's class. It was as if something tight had been tied around her neck so it hurt to swallow.

It was getting really dark now but Lucy still stubbornly sat on her suitcase. Her resolve was fading fast and she was trying to conjure up another grievance to justify her predicament.

But someone was coming along the footpath! In the gloom Lucy squinted to see who it was. It was a woman and as she approached Josie recognised Mrs. Kelly. She lived two doors down from their house and Daddy called her Mrs CT meaning "The Curtain Twitcher" because she was very nosy and always interested in everybody else's business. She was old and short and stocky with a tight bun scraped back, sharp little black eyes and always wore huge ugly cardigans which she knitted herself. Here she came, wobbling along carrying a big basket and as she approached she said, 'Good heavens child! What on earth are you doing?' Lucy wasn't going to tell Mrs Kelly a thing because she was such a nosy parker so she just said, 'Oh… I'm just sitting here having a rest Mrs Kelly. On my way home' she added as an afterthought.

'Come along then' said Mrs. Kelly so Lucy picked up her suitcase and she and Mrs Kelly walked around the corner to Lucy's path where they said good night to each other. Lucy walked up to her front door, pulled down the latch and walked in.

'Is that you Lucy?' Mummy's voice called out. 'Oh good. Your dinner's in the oven. It was getting cold.'

So Lucy sat down at the kitchen table still wearing her coat and her school hat with the elastic under her chin and her mother smiled at her as she put the plate in front of her. A huge wave of warmth rose up through Lucy's body, right up to her head 'til her cheeks were burning. She looked up.

'Eat up' Mummy said, still smiling down at her and then something lovely happened between Lucy and her mother. They both got the giggles.

RESPECTABILITY

Madeleine Briggs was sitting at her dressing table with its three oval mirrors and its collection of crystal bowls, silver trays and matching hairbrushes. Hanging nearby were a pretty silk floral dress in lilac tones and a plain linen coat in pale mauve. A pair of elegant dove grey suede shoes with modest heels were placed neatly together in front of the outfit.

She was doing her hair. She checked the centre parting. Yes...it was straight. She fluffed into soft curls the short hair framing her face. Then she brushed back her long dark hair and deftly wove it into a figure eight at the nape of her neck, stabbing it firmly in place with hair pins. She slipped on the dress, the coat, the shoes and then took her hat – the prettiest little fine straw confection, trimmed on the brim with a discreet bunch of flowers placed at ten minutes to twelve and donned it carefully at just the right angle, slightly tipped above her left eye, anchoring it firmly in place with two pearl hatpins. A jaunty piece of veiling tied in a bow completed the delightful effect, popping up vertically at the back.

Mrs Briggs set off up her street, walking lightly and briskly until she reached the village where she stood and waited for the tram. Along it came, squealing to a halt at just the right spot so she could enter via the back platform. The conductress, waiting until she had chosen a seat, tugged on the bell rope that ran the length of the tram. Off they went.

Through the village up to the top of the hill where the business district appeared below them and the harbour glinted blue in the distance. They racketed down the rise, past the gully with its old cemetery and ancient trees, turned left into Karangahape Road and then right into Queen Street.

Down the hill they sped. Past the Town Hall, the trolley sparking on the wires and the tram rocking at times, and finally into the long streets of shops and businesses. Mrs Briggs got off at Prince Albert Street, stood on the safety zone until it was clear to cross and then set off up the hill to The Farmers Emporium, in 1947 the biggest department store in the city. She was off to meet her friends for their annual Christmas high tea.

On the ground floor of The Farmers she waited for a lift. The brass plate above the lift doors was the shape of half a sun with flame like tendrils. A pointer moved slowly around, stopping as it reached each of the six floors. The door slid back, the lift attendant in her white gloves opened the rattling cage door and Mrs Briggs stepped inside.

'First floor – lingerie, nightware, ladies frocks' sang the lift attendant. She had platinum blond hair with a Victory Roll at the back and a pouffy looking arrangement in front. Her lipstick was very red indeed.

'Top floor – Tearoom' warbled the bored lift girl.

Mrs Briggs stepped out into a vast white room. The soaring arched deco roof was white hung with a row of beautiful black iron lanterns. Round islands of white tablecloths stretched left and right surrounded by bobbing hats of all varieties, nodding and turning and twisting. The din of voices was deafening.

Mrs. Briggs headed towards the northern windows. These were vast arched doors with the sun shining through them revealing the harbour beyond. Her friends were already at their usual table.

'Oh there you are! At *last*!' said Beryl. She was apparently in one of her sarcastic moods.

'Waiter!' she called. 'Our party is now complete – you can bring the tea.'

'Yes Madam' said the waiter. He had red curly hair and a matching face. He sprinted off.

Muriel and Blanche greeted Mrs Briggs in a far more welcoming manner, assuring her they too had only just arrived and telling her how nice she looked.

Her three friends, had they ever bothered to think about it at all, might have wondered where Mr Briggs might be. Mrs Briggs never spoke of him and they assumed she was a widow.

The fact was Madeleine Briggs had got rid of Mr Briggs in 1921. He drank and was violent with her. Despite her gentle and retiring demeanour she had a certain strength and stubbonness inherent in her character and so one night when he was drunk she got him to sign over the deeds of the house to her, leaving her alone with two children to bring up. Out of spite she would never agree to a divorce or to see him again but, intensely self-conscious about keeping up appearances, continued to wear her gold wedding band and five diamond engagement ring.

The high tea appeared. Translucent teacups and saucers with gold edges. A silver platter with miniature hot sausage rolls and another with fluffy white scones and jam and cream. A silver cake stand was borne in and placed as a centrepiece, piled up with colourful cakes and tarts looking like a tower of bright fruity little flowers. On the silver knob at the top was tied a bunch of holly with a red bow and, on the top tier, very neat rectangular slices of Christmas cake.

The four friends tucked in.

'Would the ladies like a complimentary sherry?'

The red faced waiter was back, beads of perspiration dotting his brow. Mrs Briggs suppressed a deep urge to hand him her handkerchief.

'Yes thank you' said Beryl sharply.

'Well I think that's very nice' said timid little Blanche.

'Yes – very' echoed Muriel. Beryl was starting to get on her nerves.

'Nonsense' snapped Beryl. 'Think of all the years we've been coming here'.

The sherry arrived in tiny glasses with silver rims. The ladies all toasted each other and took a first sip.

Goodness!' thought Mrs Briggs as an unfamiliar and pleasant warmth overtook her. 'That *is* rather nice'. She had never touched alcohol after the banishment of Mr Briggs.

Eventually everyone started to say that they must be going and began to gather their things. Then they all wove their way through the emptying tables, into the lift and descending to the ground floor they said their goodbyes and separated.

The basement floor housed produce – groceries and fresh fruit and vegetables. Mrs Briggs walked down the stairs and immediately spotted some lovely early peaches. She bought six which were put into a brown paper bag.

'Oh goodness!' thought Mrs Briggs 'I might drop them in the tram' so she bought a string bag as well and popped the bag of peaches into it.

The safety zone was very crowded and the tram even more so. Mrs Briggs had to stand and as the unfamiliar ingestion of the sherry was affecting her, she wasn't sure whether the swaying sensation was the tram or herself.

No-one offered her a seat. They all sat on the slatted wooden benches reading their newspapers or staring out the windows. Mrs. Briggs felt like a sardine packed into the standing crowd. Someone behind her was pressing in very closely which was disconcerting and people kept pushing and shoving when the tram stopped to let them on or off.

Finally, it was her stop and she squeezed her way out of the tram and onto the safety zone. The 'someone' from the tram was still right up behind her – uncomfortably close. She turned and said,

'What are you doing?' It was a man, not much taller than her who, when she turned, he turned too so that he was still behind her. She challenged him again.

'Yes Ma'am – but – just a sec' would you.....?'

She stared at him. He was flustered and red faced but he...*No*, it couldn't be! He was Mr Briggs and Mrs Briggs' string kit was somehow attached to the front of him and to her horror had caught around one of his fly buttons.

'Oh how dreadful!' she exclaimed. 'Oh how awful! I'm so sorry. Are.....?' But the man just nodded, tipped his hat and indicating no sign of recognition, hurried away towards the far end of the safety zone.

Mrs Briggs walked unsteadily down her street. All kinds of emotions overwhelmed her.

'If only the button could have been on his jacket' she muttered.

'Oh good heavens, good heavens. How embarrassing! But I'm sure it was him'. She felt rather wobbly in the knee department – a sense of shock and extreme anxiety about the disturbing encounter.

At home she undressed hastily, put on her nightgown and her dressing gown and her old comfortable slippers.

'I'll just boil a little egg' she thought 'with a nice piece of buttered toast'.

Madeleine Briggs made a big pot of sweet tea and sat down in her cosy breakfast room. She reflected on the events of the day and then suddenly, for no apparent reason, she got the giggles. They built up to a crescendo until she laughed and laughed and laughed...

A FACTORY LIFE – A MEMOIR

June in the Philippines – the wet season.

At 8am it's already 30 degrees when I sit down to breakfast out on the terrace. The cantilevered roof which protects us from all the elements thrusts forward out into the tropical garden.

Boyat the gardener is raking the dozen or so leaves that are lying on the immaculate lawn – a rhythmic soothing sound.

Mister, the Tonkanese cat sits facing out, on guard, like an elegant miniature sphinx. We are best friends, Mister and I. When Sophie and I arrive from the airport he joins the melee of humans who live in the house to greet us and when I finally go to my room to unpack and shut the door to keep the air conditioning in, he lies across my doorway – my exclusive guardian. He loves me and I love him. He is one of the few cats I can pick up without descending into a paroxysm of sneezing and I am one of the few humans that he allows to cuddle him. He's an imperial being is Mister.

Gerard, our host, is already at the table, the morning papers spread about.

Maria, the head maid appears, slippers flapping. She serves me a mango, skillfully de-stoned with the flesh artistically sliced in a geometric pattern and places my Chinese teapot beside me in its padded basket.

'morning Ma'am. No papaya this morning – it's not ripe enough. Do you want eggs?'

'morning Maria. No thanks. Just a bread roll please.'

'Okay Ma-am. Cinnamon okay?'

'Lovely. Thanks Maria.' She returns with a little basket, the warmed rolls nestled in a checked napkin.

My friend Layla, our hostess, joins us calling out to the kitchen for her orange juice and coffee and finally Sophie appears.

Many years ago Layla and I created our businesses for each other. We started designing exclusive textile products for children which she manufactured in Manila. I started importing and distributing in Australia and New Zealand on one of our bi-annual product development visits. The three of us chat a while, finish our breakfast and then we go to our rooms to change.

The driver, Mario, is polishing up our transportation. This morning it is the Company van – The Fridge On Wheels. It has the coldest aircon in Manila and no-one has ever worked out how to adjust it.

We bump our way through streets of potholes and puddles, crowds of pedestrians and clusters of squatters' huts. Colourful Jeepnies decorated with gypsy art, the primary Philippines' mode of public transport, weave their way in and out of the shambolic traffic, stopping any which way to let passengers on and off.

Arriving at the factory we jump down from the van and are hit smack in our faces with a sauna. Inside the factory isn't much better. As well as ceiling fans, huge fans like old aeroplane propellers are located on tall stands at the end of every long worktable. Linda, the head girl, greets us before we head up the stairs to the airconditioned office. The factory team, mostly women, throw surreptitious glances at us to see what we are wearing. Filipinas love fashion and Sophie and I always make an effort to dress well. It shows respect to the team of workers who put so much effort and pride into producing our products.

They have started at 7am – the workers. Many of them will have taken more than one form of transport to work. Others have moved to live nearer to the factory. Most of them are married and have numerous children, more often than not with husbands who do not work.

Upstairs Sophie settles down at her design desk. It has a glass lightbox in the centre which she can switch on to trace her designs. This factory makes our range of nursery ware – intricately appliqued baby quilts, co-ordinating bags, bibs, rattles – a myriad of textile children's items. At my desk I cost products, sort through piles of catalogues and magazines to research current international decorating trends.

I am Sophie's runner. I go up and down the stairs. To the bodega where all the fabrics are stored along with trims, ribbons etc. To the sample room to follow the progress of design development. Up and down I go – boiling one moment, sweating and then feeling chilled when I return to the office. As a result of this routine I sometimes come down with a bout of bronchitis.

The factory is filled with a gentle hum. No voices – just the whirr of the fans, the hum of sewing machines, the occasional one with a squeaky pedal. The pleasant sound of the precise noise on a wooden surface as scissors cut through layers of fabric.

At lunchtime a shrill bell rings and then the factory is filled with noise. Scraping of benches, the slapping of the girls' slippers on concrete, voices all talking and laughing at once. They surge out into the factory yard to the sari sari store where they are served sweet drinks, steaming rice-based lunches and Filipino pastries.

The factory sits behind tall concrete security walls topped with glass shards and inside the huge iron gates a container is often parked as the few young men who work in the factory load it for export. These boys also do all the screen printing, pack the products for shipment and receive and store away the heavy deliveries of fabric.

Upstairs Layla, Sophie and I tuck into lunch. What have the girls at the house packed today? In the Eski, nestled on ice we find sandwiches, salad, boiled eggs and icy cokes. Sophie and I only drink coke when we are working in the factories. Tummy upsets are a hazard and coke is the safest drink.

After lunch we settle back to work and then the electricity goes off. Brown-outs are a daily occurrence. They arrive without warning. Sometimes they last for an hour or so, sometimes for half a day. In the 1980s Manila's electricity supply does not cope and so these power cuts happen at random and without any notification. Many factories, offices and wealthy homes have their own generators – noisy filthy things that spout out diesel fumes and cause Manila to exist in a grimy fog of pollution.

Downstairs, waiting for the generator to churn up, the girls spread their arms in front of them on the worktables, lay their heads down and have a little sleep.

***

We are home. One of the housemaids brings us cool calamansi juice. We loll about on the terrace. The predictable late afternoon deluge has begun. We watch the water hurtling down the taut chains on either side of the cantilevered roof. These heavy chains extend from the end of the gutters and the water flows down into huge decorative ceramic pots which then overflow into the garden. It's lovely sitting there watching the downpour. The air feels cool – as low as 27 degrees. By this time Gerard has joined us and we all troop into the kitchen to mix our own pre dinner drinks. We eat our dinner at the table on the terrace. When we are not sleeping we live out on the terrace.

It's a strange, unusual business life that we live – unique. A lot of it is difficult and frustrating but this is our world and this house and Layla and Gerard, not only our business associates but our generous friends, virtually provide us with our second home.

THE SEARCH

Cromwell was my sister's cat. At the time she brought him home and named him she was seriously into English history. She'd found him by the stream that ran through a green space at the bottom of our hill. He was a big ginger cat with very thick fur, a fat face and a bad-tempered expression which rather reflected his namesake Oliver, without the warts. He wasn't at all affectionate even after he had settled in. He was his own man. He had a resentful air about him but he obviously thought he was onto a good thing and so he tolerated us and stayed with us for several years.

When he went missing Mum said 'Oh, he'll turn up eventually' but he didn't. After a day or two we all began to realise that we were really quite attached to him despite his negative personality. We kept listening for his grumpy meow at the back door, constantly opening it and calling out, just in case. We repeatedly searched The Tiger Country – Dad's name for the wilderness at the bottom of our garden, full of bamboo and long grasses.

On Day 3 my sister said, 'What are we going to do?'

As I was a year older than her she expected me to be proactive.

'We could make up some flyers with his name and telephone number on them.'

My sister seemed to approve of that idea so we got to work, even digging out a photo of him looking particularly brassed off. We decided we'd walk around the neighbourhood and put them in the letterboxes, but once we got started we changed our minds and knocked on doors. Mostly no-one was at home but when they were they often were elderly, possibly lonely and sometimes garrulous which provided us with a fund of stories to entertain our parents. We started to channel Alan Bennett and compose our own "Talking Heads" – in an exercise book we bought especially for the purpose.

Our first human contact had been at a house where we suspected the occupants were away. Every blind and curtain was closed tightly and the house had a 'don't you dare disturb me' air about it. It rather suited Cromwell's personality. We knocked and waited and caught a momentary glimpse of an angry face peering at us through a crack in the curtain. It closed and as we turned to leave the sound of rattling keys caught our attention. There were four locks in military precision down the front door and the person inside was obviously working their way down the line. The door opened very slowly and we were confronted by a tiny ancient woman with a walking stick. She was bent almost in half. Her short white hair grew vertically above her angry face as if sometime in the past she had experienced a terrible fright.

'What do you want?'

We explained, thrusting our flyer at her.

'Go away!' she shouted closing the door with a bang.

As we walked away we could hear the keys rattling their way down the row of deadlocks.

At No.29 there was an enormous white boat on a trailer that overwhelmed the small front garden. Behind it we could hear a lot of hammering and blasting music. We ventured cautiously around the boat to discover an open garage and a large florid man wearing a

pair of grubby shorts. Feeling nervous we tentatively held out a flyer
and at that moment a phone rang inside the house.

'Jist a mo' he said.

We looked at each other. Should we skedaddle? Before we had
made a decision he returned. He sat down on a trestle with his hands
on his beefy knees. He looked us up and down with a sort of leery
look.

'Now wot can I do for you two pretty young ladies?'

He guffawed away as if he thought this was a good joke. We
explained, gave him a flyer. He shook his head. We fled.

***

We had reached the green belt at the bottom of the hill. On the other
side was a large development of social housing. This was forbidden
territory because our parents said all kinds of rough people lived
there. We surveyed it. My sister said, 'Should we go over there?'

I was doubtful but anything seemed worth a try. We walked across
the grass and the little bridge which straddled the stream where my
sister had first met Cromwell.

The houses on this side were very different. Their front yards
were full of rubbish - old pieces of machinery, abandoned vehicles
without wheels, filthy mattresses, broken strollers, beer bottles.

We hesitated – doubtful.

My sister said, 'Oh, at least let's give *this* one a try'.

The house looked a tad better than most of the others with a
bright display of marigolds populated by a gaggle of garden gnomes.
Attached to the front wall there was a huge pastel wooden butterfly
with No 12 painted on it. This seemed to hint at a degree of domestic

pride. We knocked. The door was opened by an enormous woman with a cheery smile.

'Gidday Girls!' she beamed. 'Wot's your story eh?'

We explained, offering her a flyer.

'Righto!' she said, ignoring it. 'Well, I 'avent't seen 'im but I'll get a pen.'

She disappeared for a short while. We surveyed the passage. It displayed a riotous floral wallpaper, bruised and battered and through the door at the far end we could see a kitchen with the sink piled up with the unwashed detritus of countless meals.

The woman returned with a pen. Ignoring our flyer she asked, 'Now wot's y'number lovelies?' We told her and she ripped a piece of wallpaper off the wall and wrote the number on the back.

'I'll keep an eye out for 'im kiddos. Doncha worry. Good luck!'

'I think she will' my sister remarked as we trailed home. 'In fact I think she's most likely the kindest one of them all. She's our only hope!'

We didn't tell our parents that we'd been down to the social housing and Cromwell never returned. A few months later, after what we considered to be a suitable time to respect his memory, we visited The Pound and got a dog.

THE BAY

1950

The Bay lies silent and still in the early morning – waiting. Gentle waves roll softly onto the sand, back and forth, back and forth. Beyond the beach the sea is pale grey/blue and glassy and far away misty islands float on a colourless ocean. The gnarled pohutukawa trees lean protectively over the back of the beach, clinging to the cliffs, throwing dense shadows onto the sand, their brilliant red flowers are like little round fluffy brushes. Up on the high cliffs at each end of the bay the silence is broken by the beautiful bell-like warble of a tui. On the sand three little sailing dinghies lie stranded at various angles above the waterline. The beach waits for the day to begin.

Down the cliff path strides John Dennison wearing his old rugby shorts and a towel slung over his shoulder. Into the sea he plunges, disappearing and then swooping up, standing waist deep, shaking the water from his hair, rubbing his face. Then he plunges in again and begins to swim along the length of The Bay, his thin body a long, submerged vessel, his head the bow and his arms driving him along at an even rhythm with a little white splash of spray at the stern where his feet are kicking. The wake behind him forms a dark line which slowly dissolves and returns to a glassy surface. John Dennison swims his two lengths of The Bay, wades back to the beach, picks up his towel and goes home for breakfast.

The Bay is silent again, waiting, except for a solitary fish that leaps and plops. A silver flash in the blink of an eyelid.

As the sun creeps up the beach and the shade of the trees recedes, young voices can be heard in the distance. They come closer, laughing and bickering. There is one amateur whistler. They flush down the boat ramp and out onto the sand – three young boys.

'C'mon...let's put the boats in.'

'There's no wind.'

'Oh, who cares. We can row for a while. Let's see if we can sink 'Marylou.'

They drag the clinker built twelve-footer into the water and all jump in. They rock the boat sideways – violently back and forth so that water rushes in. The eldest boy, twelve-year-old Jack Streatfield, grabs the bailer that is floating around and starts sloshing more seawater into the boat. It steadily fills up until only the gunwale is visible and the occupants are sitting in water up to their waists.

'That's it,' yells Jack. 'It's never going to sink because of the buoyancy tanks.'

They all jump out, wading and towing the boat back to the beach and onto firm sand, tipping it onto its side to let the water pour out.

***

In the house on top of the cliff at the northern end of The Bay, Lucy, still in bed, stirs stretches listens. She sits up. Through the window the forest of huge fragrant pines surrounding the house are at attention, shady and green. The meat safe hanging from a branch on its rope is motionless in the still morning with a few frustrated flies hovering around it. Lucy dresses, bathing suit first then shorts and shirt on top. She chooses a towel and pops into the kitchen where her mother is sitting at the board table with toast and tea. Lucy kisses Louise Laurence on her forehead, grabs two pieces of toast and disappears out the door.

'Did you clean your teeth?' Her mother calls after her but she pretends not to hear and runs on through the pine forest and starts to skidder down the track to the beach below. She passes The Cove and notes the tide is in. Great! She reaches the beach where the boys are preparing the sails on the boats. A tentative little breeze has sprung up and they're keen to go.

'The tide's in at The Cove' she announces. 'Let's swim.'

The boys look at each other, undecided. As usual Jack takes the lead.

'Okay. Leave the sails furled' he instructs his eleven-year-old brother Roger and their friend Andy Dennison.

They all race along the beach and up the cliff path then plunge down into The Cove. It is full of water which is lapping precisely level with the rock ledge. They hurl themselves in and splash and swim around, the boys wrestling and ducking each other under water. Lucy swims and treads water, watching them warily and dodging them when they get too close. Really, they are *so* ridiculous at times.

Ten minutes later they are clambering out and racing back to the beach. The boys get busy setting the sails and, as the wind is increasing, they launch the three boats into the water.

'Who am I going with?' asks Lucy hopefully. The boys look doubtful. Lucy's considered a bit of a liability where sailing is concerned. Eventually Roger reluctantly volunteers and they set sail.

'You can hold the mainsheet' offers Roger graciously. He's at the tiller. He hands Lucy the rope and she feels very proud. Usually, if they even agree to take her she just has to sit there as a passenger. She seriously concentrates, holding onto the rope tightly, looking upwards at the tension in the sail and feeling happy and responsible. The three little sailing boats bob around The Bay, wheeling and tacking back and forth. The strict rules are 'Don't sail past the Points' which are the two headlands that guard each end of The Bay and they all comply as any disobedience means all three boats are grounded for three days no matter who the transgressor might be.

'Going about!' yells Roger suddenly, pushing the tiller to starboard. Taken by surprise Lucy is too slow to duck as the boat changes course and the wind grabs the sail so that the boom swings around and hits her on the head – *BANG*! She is seeing stars! She has let go of the rope.

'Are you okay?' from Roger. The other two boys are looking over and rolling their eyes. Lucy says she's alright but slumps down on the seat holding her aching head. Roger takes the rope and skilfully turns the boat towards the shore and the three boys sail their yachts into the shallows and drag them up well above the waterline. They start chasing each other in and out of the water and racing around the beach, wrestling and shouting.

Lucy sits on the soft sand in the shade nursing her very painful head. There seems to be a substantial bump growing on her forehead. To her right the cliff pushes forward into the sea and at the base there are wide flat rocks where a myriad of rock pools are revealed at low tide sheltering small salty creatures – sea anemones, hermit crabs in their little shell houses and tiny shrimps. At full tide the rocks are completely submerged and in rough weather the waves hurl themselves against the cliffs, assaulting and retreating.

To her left is her cliff with its blanket of dark green pines and The Cove below it. Beyond The Cove at low tide there are lots more flat rocks stretching far along the coastline with rock pools decorated with oysters, mussels and in sandy places, cockles. The children sometimes roam along these rocks at low tide and then climb up the steep cliffs and walk back along the top of the escarpment to the Laurences' beach house.

Lucy is now eleven and remembers very well the first time they came here. There was a polio epidemic after The War had finished and Dad decided they must get out of the city. He found the little holiday house on the cliff above this remote bay, far from danger. Walter Laurence packed up his family – Mummy, Grand, baby Nella and Lucy and brought them here until the summer was well over and he judged it safe for them to return to the city. Lucy even missed quite a few weeks of school that year which was super.

She remembered that Dad borrowed someone's car and that it was a Model-T Ford for heaven's sake! They drove onto the vehicular ferry to cross the harbour before they set off on that first long drive to The Bay. It was *so* embarrassing because Dad was worried the old car wouldn't start when they were ready to drive off the ferry at the other end and it would be unthinkable to delay other vehicles from disembarking. So inconsiderate. He had to start the car by winding a big metal handle at the front and so, to be on the safe side he kept the motor running all the way across the harbour and the car jiggled up and down and rattled and the motor made a lot of noise. It also had smelly smoke blowing out the back. It was utterly humiliating.

How they ever managed to reach The Bay in that old bomb she would never know. It took simply a million hours and the road was so windy and bumpy and dusty.

Mummy loved the beach and swimming. She was a very good swimmer and could go on for what seemed like hours doing The Crawl so they spent most of their time on the beach provided the weather was nice. One day, on their way down the cliff path and past The Cove they discovered a little fairy penguin all on its own, sitting sadly on the rock ledge. While they were looking at it and wondering what to do a lady and her son who looked to be about the same age as Lucy appeared and they were Mrs Dennison and Andy. And that was how the three families got together at The Bay. Their annual summer holidays had been bliss ever since. Lucy couldn't help feeling grateful to the polio epidemic.

A bell rings high up on Lucy's cliff. Lunchtime. The boys hurtle off in their different directions yelling 'Bye'...

'Bye... see ya.'

'Okay! See ya this arvo...'

They disappear and Lucy too sets off for home and lunch and hopefully yummy sandwiches filled with great chunky slices of the Christmas ham that is stored in the meat safe. She hopes Dad has already done the carving because there often tends to be a major crisis when the ham is being transported from the meat safe into the kitchen. Blowflies are really tricky and nip inside so fast and Dad gets really uptight when they are whizzing around the kitchen because they are so unhygienic. And Mum is *really* vicious when she tears around with the fly swat. Even if she misses one she bashes at the surfaces so violently it's possible any surviving fly would suffer a concussion. Lucy feels her forehead again. Ouch! That bump appears to be growing.

Below the house the sand stirs in the wind. The tide turns. The waves are busier and more important. The Bay settles down again and waits.

***

It's early afternoon. Lots of people are approaching the beach. First come the Dennisons, John and his wife Jacqueline with Andy tagging along eating a banana. Then here come the Streatfields – Larry and Diana with Jack and Roger in tow. Finally the Laurences – Walter and Louise with their girls Lucy and Nella and Mrs Briggs, Louise's mother. The adults lay out towels on the sand and all sit or lie about sunbathing and chatting. Mrs Briggs sits in a folding chair with a sunshade. She is wearing a pretty lilac floral dress and a wide brimmed hat to match. The men smoke. The children all disperse to embark on a major architectural construction in the ideally damp firm sand left by the outgoing tide. The boys have brought serious looking spades and in no time a fort takes shape with a moat around it and a drainage channel down to the water's edge. Nella, who is only little, potters importantly back and forth to the building site, delivering shells and seaweed and some dandelions she has found growing a little way up the bank.

'Look here Nella. Forts don't have flowers!' Jack is at that moment in charge of the complex construction of the artillery battery, giving orders to Roger and Andy.

'But I *want* to' wails Nella. 'Mummy, why can't I put flowers on the castle?'

Diana Streatfield chips in.

'Jack – let Nella place her flowers. She's just a little mite. Be a bit more tolerant'. Jack pulls a face when he thinks she isn't looking.

'I don't know...' drawls Diana who hasn't missed the look. 'What a lovely day though ...' She is a tall thin woman, eccentric in her own unique way. She gives the impression of vagueness with her languid manner but this is deceptive. Today she is wearing a rather smart navy and white print sundress topped with her usual very battered old straw sunhat with torn holes and fraying on the brim which enables patches of sunlight to encroach and throw flashes of light onto her face. The hat is trimmed around the crown with a chain of the multi-coloured plastic rings that are usually put on chicken's legs. However, despite this unusual fashion statement she still manages to look elegant. Her sons Jack and Roger on the other hand always look extremely dorky during the six weeks of the summer holidays because as soon as they arrive at the beach their mother puts a pudding basin on their heads and cuts their hair straight around the rim. They look like a couple of rather disreputable monks.

The afternoon ambles on, the shadows grow longer, the tide has turned and is threatening the fort. The families start packing up their towels and beach paraphernalia and set off for home.

'Goodbye! Goodbye! Drinks at 5.30 at our place – okay?

'Righto. See you then.'

The soft sand on the beach is all tumbled and tossed. The tide rolls in to smooth it out. The sea sighs. The Bay slumbers.

***

'Wait for me! Hey – wait for me!' Nella's soft little feet step gingerly over the rocks which are slimy and slippery in places. She wobbles and edges cautiously around the rock pools and the crusty oysters.

'Oh *please* wait for me!' Past The Cove where the tide is out and the cave revealed, the others are well ahead of her, swinging their buckets and stepping over the rocks with ease. They turn and Lucy runs back and takes Nella's hand.

'You shouldn't have come' she says. 'We told you not to come because you can't keep up'.

'But I *want* to'. Nella's rosy little face pouts, her blond curls are plastered on her forehead and her shorts are wet and clinging to her firm little bottom.

'It's not fair' she puffs as Lucy drags her along. 'Just 'cos I'm nearly four you shouldn't leave me out when I've got legs'. 'No,' she mutters to herself. 'It's difnitly not fair'.

Lucy slows down.

'Come on – we can catch up'. The boys have stopped now at a sandy place and are crouching down digging away and putting cockles into their buckets. The parents have sent them out and the children are happy to go. Cockles mean a party in the evening which means they can stay up late but they have to work fast before the tide turns.

'I can do it! I can do it!' cries Nella digging her little fingers into the firm wet sand and finding nothing. With her bottom facing upwards her shorts are decorated with a soggy assortment of beachy material collected when she fell down along the way.

'Look' Lucy tells her. 'You need to search for little holes and bubbles in the sand. That's the clue because that's where the cockles breath'. Nella looks and spies one. She digs fiercely, her face red with exertion. At last! A cockle!

'I've got one! I found one! Look Roger! Look Jack! Look Andy!' Everyone looks and praises and then gets back to digging. They fill the buckets and set off back towards the beach. They deliver the bounty to the Streatfields' bach. It has a lawn so all outdoor parties tend to be held there. They've also got the best Long Drop. It's in a hedge and is permanent. The other two fathers have to dig a new temporary one every year when they arrive. If anyone needs 'to go' while they are at the Streatfields they don't have to yoohoo as they approach to warn anyone who might already be ensconced. All they need to do is listen because they can hear the person inside slapping and swearing due to a proliferation of mosquitoes.

Diana Streatfield is on the porch sweeping. As they approach they hear her exclaim, 'Drat those bloody birds. They've shat all over the verandah'. The delivery contingent pretend not to hear. Verandah! That battered old thing! Honestly, no-one could call it a verandah! The Streatfield's beach house, even with a lawn *and* a permanent Long Drop, is the most humpty-doo of all the houses at The Bay.

When she gets home Lucy asks her mother what 'shat' means.

'In what context?' Louise enquires.

'Well, we just took the cockles to the Streatfield's and Mrs. Streatfield said the birds had shat on the porch'.

'Oh, that means bird pooh' her mother replies dismissively. She's a bit preoccupied preparing big slabs of brown bread and butter ready for the cockle party and she already has an apple pie baking to take for dessert. Nella, munching on a piece of bread and butter is ecstatic.

'Bird pooh! Bird pooh! Poohy poo poo'.

'Stop it Nella' says her mother absentmindedly. 'That's enough'.

'Poohy poo poo' Nella whispers with a sly glance at her mother who ignores her.

Lucy goes and lies on her bed with a book. She has brought the latest Enid Blyton with her plus her favourite 'Anne of Green Gables' and she knows she is going to get an assortment of rather more grownup books for Christmas, censored by her mother. Authors called Elizabeth Goudge and Georgette Heyer apparently and a book called 'I Capture the Castle' by Dodie Smith (funny name - Dodie).

She reads until her father pops his head around the door and says it's time to go. Her father Walter is extremely handsome. In fact Lucy thinks he is the most handsome man she has ever seen – so far. She is very proud of her parents and is always excited when she introduces them to any of her friends. Her mother isn't exactly beautiful – just pretty sometimes when she is dressed up. But because she is so friendly and pleasant and smiley she mostly *appears* to be pretty and she has millions of friends which is very impressive.

The Laurence family drive over to the Streatfields' because it's a bit far for Grand to walk even though she is still very sprightly but also it will be dark by the time they come home. When they arrive the three families all sit around on the lawn, the adults on garden chairs and the children on rugs. The cockles have been boiled until their shells have opened just a smidgen after which the water is drained and they are put back in the buckets and brought out steaming hot. They are served with vinegar (if you like it) and with the big slabs of fresh brown bread and butter. The men drink beer and the women gin and tonic or perhaps a Pimms or sometimes a shandy which is beer and lemonade mixed together. Mrs Briggs is persuaded to take a small sherry. The children are allowed to taste the grown ups' drinks (just a sip) but the lemonade is wizard. Jacqueline Dennison has brought her ukulele so they all have a sing song and the children stand up and recite a poem or sing a solo song – that is, if they are any good at it.

The Dads are talking a lot about whitebaiting. It's the season so they are making preparations. First of all they have to organise the bait. This involves taking a big long drag net down to the beach when the tide is right and stretching it along in the shallows to catch sprats. These are small fish and the poor little things are taken home and minced up (after they are dead fortunately) to make berley. Then on a night when the weather is calm and preferably a full moon, the men go out in the fishing dingy with the bucket of berley as bait which they throw into the water around the boat, lower a lantern and wait for the whitebait to turn up, attracted to the light. They catch them in small close woven nets on poles. They are tiny translucent white fish with a friendly black eye and everyone absolutely loves them because Louise just tosses them in some flour then into some beaten egg and quickly makes them into fritters. Too delicious. The party breaks up when it starts to get a bit chilly and breezy and everyone goes home.

Down on the beach a wind is arriving. It stirs the pohutukawas, strengthens and then blows some of the red flowers off the trees. The water is restless and begins to ruffle and peak and roll. Clouds soon fill the sky and there are no stars. A storm is brewing. The Bay waits.

In the three baches the families sleep, dry and cosy.

***

Lucy wakes. It's definitely morning but so dark! It's raining. A strong wind is tossing the pine trees back and forth and the meat safe is wildly swinging to and fro.

Damn!' thinks Lucy (a forbidden word). 'Now what can we all do today?' It's cold so she actually remembers to put on her dressing gown and then she pads out into the kitchen in her bare feet.

'Where are your slippers?' She retrieves her slippers and returns.

'What's for breakfast?'

'Bacon and eggs – poached or fried?'

'Poached please. Oh what are we going to do today? It's so boring when it's like this.'

'We haven't put the Christmas Tree up yet. Daddy cut a really nice branch. It's in the garage.

'Brilliant!' I'll ask the boys to come over and help decorate. They always like to do that'.

This is true. The Streatfields and the Dennisons don't bother with Christmas trees so every year their sons go over to the Laurences' to help set theirs up. It is the perfect place with all those pine trees around it. Never any difficulty of finding a suitable tree there. Jack, Roger and Andy secretly love decorating the tree although they would never admit it because it's not exactly a boy thing. They try to give the impression that they are doing the Laurences a big favour.

There are no telephones in any of the baches. They have to use the phone box up next to the General Store. But that's no problem. That's why the Laurences have The Bell. It was once a school bell so it's really loud. The children can hear it from anywhere in The Bay and the three families long ago agreed on synchronised meal times. It's attached to the garage wall so Lucy runs out into the rain and rings the bell for ages. The wind is wild and loud so she hopes it will carry the sound in the right direction. It does. Within what seems like minutes the three boys arrive, panting, dripping wet and sandy having taken the shortcut along the beach and up the cliff past The Cove. They dry off using the Laurences' tattiest old towels, drink some Ovaltine that Mrs Laurence gives them to warm them up and then everyone dives into the big bags, eventually tipping them upside down to speed things up. Christmas balls, tinsel, an assortment of all sorts of glittery things including a large star tumble out onto the floor and everyone starts decorating. Mr Laurence brings in a ladder.

'I'll do the top branches' Jack announces which is no surprise to anyone. 'I'm the oldest and the tallest so it's best I handle the dangerous jobs'. Everyone rolls their eyes. He climbs the ladder and plonks the star on the top of the tree.

'Yes – you're the biggest' says Nella. 'But what about me when I'm the littlest?' She picks up a shiny red bauble and waves it about.

'You can do the bottom branches' says Lucy reassuringly. 'Look. This is how you attach it.'

Nella fumbles and inevitably drops the bauble which shatters into a myriad of tiny pieces. She starts to wail – loudly. Andy, who has been decorating around the other side of the tree and discreetly practising his whistling, appears with a ball exactly the same as the broken one. He has actually already spent quite a long time attaching it but he's a kind boy and doesn't like to see Nella so distressed. Admittedly she's a bit of a drag at times but she's only little and deserves a break now and then. He's eleven and an only child and would rather like to have a little sister or brother as his home life tends to be rather quiet and uneventful. The Laurences and the Streatfields always seem to be *doing* things and he thinks he'd rather like that even if it must get a bit tiring at times. He admires Mr Laurence enormously. If it wasn't for him Dad would never have bought him his sailing boat. He helps

Nella attach the bauble and she immediately becomes his slave and insists on helping him with every single decoration until the tree is finished which, Andy must admit, really *does* become a bit of a drag.

Eventually they are finished and they all stand back and admire their work. They make a few adjustments here and there.

'My goodness!' exclaims Mrs Briggs. 'That's perfect. I really think it is the very best tree you have ever done'. She disappears back into the kitchen where she and Louise are serving up hot meat pies. This is a huge surprise and greeted with overwhelming enthusiasm by the decorating team who, once they have polished off every pie, pile into the kitchen to thank the caterers.

Roger says, 'Jack – with this rough weather I'm a bit worried about the boats. Do you think we should go down and check that they are still safely above the waterline? The rain has stopped'. Jack looks authoritative and after a theatrical moment of pondering finally announces that he thinks they should go and check on the boats as if it had been his idea. Everyone decides to go except Nella who fortunately is having her afternoon sleep. She's worn out after all the excitement and the tears and the meat pie (only half) has slowed her down somewhat. It was a bit of a sinker, particularly when she'd had a 'normus bowl of porridge for breakfast.

Lucy, Jack, Roger and Andy set off down the cliff path, past The Cove where the sea at full tide is smashing over the rock ledge, hitting the cliff face and splashing back again in a whirlwind of foam. The gale is very strong while they are up high but less forceful once they are down on the beach. The three little boats are sitting safely on dry sand but the boys drag them right up to the cliff just to be on the safe side. They hook the anchors around the pohutukawa roots.

The four friends sit down at the back of the beach close to the cliff bank.

'It's not a Spring Tide is it?' asks Andy anxiously. Jack reckons it's not. 'I don't *think* so'. Actually he hasn't noticed whether the moon has been a crescent or full. They watch the waves rolling in. Strewn along the beach at the high water mark is a thick heap of seaweed, brown and slimy with little round brown berries which squirt water when they are squeezed. The waves are still thrusting more up onto the sand. Every now and then a really big wave comes crashing in and the wind catches the foam and flings it forward so the children can feel a fine spray on their faces.

Suddenly, to their surprise, down the boat ramp come two ladies.

'Hello Aunts' calls Jack.

They are Fillida and Lilian, Diana Streatfield's twin sisters, known affectionately in the family as Fil and Lil. They are wearing dressing gowns with bathing suits underneath. Both are wearing white rubber bathing caps.

'It's a bit wild to be going for a swim' suggests Jack.

'Oh no dear' Lil replies, taking off her dressing gown. 'We're made of tough stuff, aren't we dear?' shouting to Fil who is going deaf. She is also shedding her dressing gown revealing a very old sagging elasticised bathing suit. The two women teeter over the seaweed and wade into the water. They dive under an incoming wave, their two white caps emerging on the other side. The children watch them bobbing and swimming about in the turbulent water. They seem to be enjoying it. Fil turns towards the oncoming waves and starts to swim out when suddenly an enormous wave rolls in smashing into her head-on. She disappears for a moment then appears again, surfing towards the water's edge. She stands up and her bathing suit has sagged right down in the front revealing a pair of equally sagging bosoms. The children start yelling, 'Aunty Fil – your togs have come down!' but their voices are carried away by the wind.

Fil nods, smiles, waves, turns and dives in again. The children are rolling around on the sand. They can't stop laughing it's so hilarious. Roger decides to be responsible and runs down to the water's edge. He waits for Fil to emerge again and makes hitching movements with his arms. She can't hear him and nods, smiles, waves before turning again and diving in.

Lucy picks up Fil's dressing gown and waits in the shallows. The two sisters eventually have had enough and start to wade ashore where Fil, surprised, graciously accepts the garment from Lucy and puts it on. Roger has had the forethought to bring Lil's gown as well just so it won't appear as if they are playing favourites. Blithely unaware Fil potters back up the beach and the two aunts disappear up the boat ramp, chattering to each other and leaving the young onlookers rolling around on the sand in hysterics. It really will be an event that they will replay over and over in the future when they are all together and want a good laugh.

'What'll we do now?' asks Roger.

'Do you wanna play ping pong?' suggests Andy. The Dennisons have recently put a table in their garage. Everyone agrees to this plan and they take a short cut by climbing up the bank via the tree roots.

The waves continue to roll in – big ones, smaller ones. The wind whips up the spray. The seaweed lies in dense brown islands, rocking back and forth in the swell. Immaculate black and white seagulls strut around on the sand, their feathers ruffled in the wind. They fly up and wheel around, riding on the gusts of wind and diving down again onto the surface of the water where they float composedly up and down with the movement of the waves. Slowly the storm moves away. The Bay sighs and rests.

***

It's a lovely morning – sunny and at 10 o'clock, already warm.

'I'm off' Lucy says to her mother who kisses her and plonks a sunhat on her head saying, 'It's going to be hot so stay in the shade. You've already lost enough skin off your nose so keep your hat on. I'll be bringing Nella down for a swim later. See you then'.

Lucy scoots down the cliff path and onto the beach. Not a soul to be seen! The three little sailing boats are sitting dry above the water line. Strange! Such a lovely day and a nice little breeze – you'd think the boys would be out sailing already.

Lucy sits down on the sand to wait and then suddenly she hears voices and the strange sound of repetitive groaning and growling and the unfamiliar sound of a motor starting up in a grunting, gurgling sort of way. She clambers up the cliff onto the dirt road and there, parked under the trees like some gigantic metallic praying mantis, is the elusive grader with Jack in the cabin and Roger and Andy standing on the road grinning up at him. The huge orange vehicle with its long extended arms supporting the scoop and its quaint little cabin with windows at the back is stationary but vibrating up and down as its motor settles into a steady growl. Seldom actually spotted it is always the subject of discussion on the interminable drive to and from The Bay. Daddy will get really angry as they judder over the corrugated surface.

129

'My God! This road is worse than ever! When will they put the grader through!' or 'It's not so bad this year – the grader must have just been through.' So, at last this mysterious being has materialised!

'Don't Jack!' Lucy yells up at him. 'Turn it off! It's dangerous!'

Jack ignores her. He's really enjoying himself with a big smirk on his face.

Lucy, terrified, shrieks

'Stop it Jack! Stop it! What if it moves? It might go over the cliff!'

To Roger and Andy, standing on the road hooting away and spurring Jack on, she implores, 'Stop him – *please!*'

Jack makes a big thing of extending his feeling of command by importantly pretending to test the implements in the cabin but finally he turns off the engine and the grader gives one final almighty shudder and lapses into silence. He leaps to the ground and the three boys clear off down to the beach, laughing and chortling and thinking they are hugely daring. Lucy sighs and follows them. Her legs feel a bit wobbly. '*Honestly!* They're the pits at times.'

***

The moon is full. The Spring Tide is high and calm. The Bay is all black and golden. It is a warm night so the four friends have come down to the beach after dinner for a swim. They love to swim at night. The phosphorescence with its illuminated silver bubbles rises to the surface when they flail their arms around. It's magical. They swish around for quite a while and then run up the beach, dry off and sit down on their towels. The Bay looks so beautiful and the moon and stars are throwing down so much light they can clearly see the Dennisons' dingy that is used for fishing rocking gently on its anchor chain.

Jack and Roger's father, Larry Streatfield comes walking down the ramp. He doesn't see the children sitting up in the shadows at the back of the beach. He drops his towel on the sand, takes off his clothes and wades into the water. He sets off swimming strongly towards the moored dingy where he takes out his false teeth, placing them under the seat at the stern. He then sets off swimming quite far out and starts traversing The Bay, back and forth.

Suddenly here comes John Dennison. He is carrying an inflated lilo and a towel with him. He takes off his clothes, puts them on the lilo and sets off kicking and pushing it in front of him. He reaches the dingy, hoists himself up over the gunwale, stands and towels himself dry, puts on his clothes, sits down setting the oars in the rowlocks and starts rowing towards the southern headland, towing the lilo. He's off to throw a line over in a good fishing spot he knows about.

The children sit there. Will they call out? Should they tell him that Larry Streatfield's teeth are under the seat? No – it's far too funny. They say nothing. They just quietly pick up their towels and go home.

***

'Now where are my sandshoes? Oh – there they are. Why did I put them there for heaven's sake!' Louise Laurence is looking a bit frazzled as today their summer holiday is over and they are closing up the house to return to the city for Lucy to start the new school year. The Streatfields and Dennisons have already gone.

Walter is packing the car. He's *really* good at it provided he has everything marshalled together before he begins. Lucy seems organised and, as always Grand is very organised. He's got all his stuff together too so now there's just Nella's conglomeration of toys and bits and pieces important only to her. Louise has the worst of it so he goes inside to see how he can help.

Eventually the car is packed and everyone gets in – Grand and the two girls in the back with Walter driving and Louise beside him. They slowly edge along the narrow winding track through the pine forest. Lucy won't look back. Already she has that dreaded 'leaving The Bay' lump developing in her throat. They drive along the dirt road that skirts above The Bay. She can't look down. She mustn't look down She can't bear it – the lump is getting bigger and she can feel her eyes welling up.

Now they are on the peninsular road, juddering over the corrugated surface with a cloud of white dust following their progress. On both sides of the peninsular the bright blue water sparkles up at them, showing off and emphasizing all that they are leaving. They pass the lonely little white timber church on the hill and turn the corner that takes them off the peninsular. The interminably long bumpy drive stretches ahead of them. Lucy can't control the lump any longer. The tears begin to roll down her cheeks. She turns her head and rests her forehead against the car window.

Behind them The Bay lies deserted. Gentle waves roll in and out, in and out. The small salty creatures continue their short lives – underneath the sand, in the rock pools, beneath the water. The three sailing boats and the fishing dinghy have gone – towed up to their respective houses. The pohutukawa flowers have long fallen, their fluffy scarlet brushes faded to pink then to brown. are now invisible, merged with the sand.

All are waiting. The Bay is waiting.

IVY AND QUEEN MARY

A storm appeared to be brewing. Glancing out the window across the burnt crusty lawn she saw great grey clouds moving forward into the endless blue sky, cooling the hot air with a tiny breeze and the occasional hopeful gust of wind. Thunder boomed and rattled and a couple of mighty cracks threw down some heavy rain and hail. It was brief. No substance. At the end of a searing hot Australian summer, a disappointment.

She returned her gaze to the television. The movie had ended. The title music ambled its way to its finale as the credits rolled on and on up the screen. And suddenly, for no reason she began to cry. She cried as she hadn't cried for years. Really seriously serious crying, from the gut throughout all her body. Great heaving sobs of unbearable grief.

She cried for her past, her youth and the end of her productive self-fulfilling working life which she had so loved. She cried for her mistakes, her widowhood, her mothering failures, her family, her loss of youthful energy, her longing to be once more productive, busy, travelling, useful, loved, praised, looking forward not back. For the fact was she hated being old. From the depths of her soul she hated it which was, she knew, fruitless. A pathetic waste of time.

'Get yourself out of the chair. Put down the book. Turn off the television. That ivy needs trimming back.'

Out she goes in full gardening gear. She's on the job, secateurs snipping, lots of bending over. Her thoughts wander. Ivy. Queen Mary's nemesis. How does she know that? She read it somewhere. Or was it in a documentary? She remembers Queen Mary. She was The Queen's paternal grandmother and attended her wedding to Prince Philip in 1947, viewing the ceremony through a lorgnette. Regally erect and corseted, QM would have needed serious structural reinforcement to support all those jewels.

'Ah, good. I've collected a substantial tangly clump. Into the green bin it goes.'

***

There wasn't any ivy in the London garden, the front one being small and neat. Just a lawn dotted with daisies and a fine English oak shading the paved path that led to the front door with its two white painted stone lions on guard.

They lived on a lane. Well, it had been a lane when she lived there. She guessed now that it was quite a busy road. She knew this because recently she had found the house on the internet looking the same but with an extension on the side where the garage used to be. The 'lane' now had a yellow painted double line down the middle which suggested that these days there must be lots of traffic.

After arriving in London they had found the house quite quickly. Someone they knew had been told about a lovely flat for rent in the Wimbledon area. She was dead against it. In the suburbs? No!

But one day there they were, off the train and walking along the lane which displayed, on their side of the road, a row of identical faux Arts and Crafts semi-detached houses. Her husband had the house number in his pocket and assured her that they were 'on the right side'. The houses on the other side were of assorted periods - quite an architectural selection. As they walked on for what seemed to be ages and she was getting crosser and crosser, they saw opposite a lovely Victorian house which stood out amongst the other houses. She wished so much that it could be their house. And it was! Her husband pulled the note out of his pocket and **what** a surprise! They were on the wrong side of the road and yes, 206 – it was the one!

Up the path they went. The front door opened and a woman burst out saying, 'Oh, come inside! How lovely to meet you!' And so of course they took the flat which the owners rented to them because they liked them.

'Oh drat! Where have those secateurs gone? I bought hot pink so they would stand out Ah! Here they are – buried in the ivy.'

Apparently, the formidable Queen Mary, once she had been widowed, used to visit reluctant friends for extended periods of time and if she spotted any ivy in their gardens, commanded them to remove it.

Yes – London had been a highlight in their expatriate life. And Hong Kong. Ah, Hong Kong! During their tenure not overloaded with those shiny towers of offices which these days are lit in varying colours of moving lights and are now viewed at night through a permanent haze of pollution. It was the sixties and they had lived on The Island beside one of the 19th century walking pathways that wandered through lovely woodlands between mellow stone walls. Little creatures – lizards and insects inhabited the walls and huge butterflies flew free in the warm seasons. Occasionally a pheasant would cross the path.

The harbour humming below was teaming with an amazing variety of vessels. Cargo ships, little sampans, huge, wonderful junks with faded pink sails and the iconic Star Ferries. Not now. Relentless land reclamation had transformed the harbour into a narrow channel with a dangerous current. No longer Safe Harbour.

***

So many countries, so many lives, so many people and places. She had lived in the best of times. How lovely it had been.

'There! That should do for today. Suddenly I'm very tired. I'll dump the last clump into the bin. Might as well wheel it out to the gate now ready for the week's collection – it's full. Whew it's heavy. Soldier on girl – just a little bit further...

She falls. Onto an English lawn dotted with daisies. So soft. So green. The great oak beside the paved path rearranges its Spring leaves to protect and shade her. She glimpses the sky. An ethereal junk sails majestically through diaphanous clouds in an infinite blue.

That eternal sky. The only observer to witness the precious life that had been exclusively hers.

PARTY BOYS

It was December and Christmas parties were starting. Young people, old people – that is parents. All were getting together in houses, halls, clubs and offices to begin to celebrate the festive season.

In 1956 Lucy Laurence was seventeen. She already had a job at a travel agency. Besides being a stenographer/secretary to Mr Forster, a chain smoker, who planned the travel tours in a poky, permanently hazy office where she would type up all the itineraries on a manual typewriter, Lucy was also the Meet and Greet person. She would escort the tour parties to the airport and was responsible for all their travel documents, nannying them right up to departure time when she stood out on the tarmac as they tottered up the stairs onto the aircraft clutching their travel wallets and cabin bags. When they reached the aircraft door they'd turn around to wave to their friends and relatives who were up on the outdoor observation deck and Lucy would wave frantically as well. She loved her job.

With Christmas approaching there were lots of parties within the small group of airlines and travel agencies that existed at that time. Travel, particularly long-haul air travel, was still pretty exclusive in the fifties. Living in the Antipodes, people mostly went overseas on ships.

One of the airlines was giving a Christmas party and Lucy was going out with one of the boys in Reservations. They weren't going steady or anything like that, just dating casually. His name was Alan

Crichton. He invited Lucy to be his date and she said yes. They were joined by two of Alan's friends – Freddy Shaw and Barry Spender. Lucy was picked up at her house by Alan who came in and greeted her parents, as escorts did in those days.

Alan had a very old Austin-7 – a tin can on wheels with no grunt whatsoever. In fact, it was so bad on hills that the three boys would sometimes take it out on a Sunday for a bit of a lark which involved parking at the bottom of a long steep hill until a line of cars came along and then pulling out in front of them and creeping slowly up the hill as the Austin lost less and less power. The person in the back seat would count how many cars they had accumulated in the queue and, whatever the final count was, it equalled the number of beers Crichton, Shaw and Spender would put away later at the pub.

The party was held in one of the airport hangers and was in full swing when they arrived. As the evening wore on, Lucy, who didn't drink because she didn't like it – although occasionally a Pimms was okay - started to feel exhausted. It was so noisy because everyone was shouting over the loud music but it didn't matter to them as most of them had had a lot to drink and weren't listening anyway.

Eventually she sought out Alan and told him she'd like to go home. He was hooting away in a group, cigarette and glass of beer in his left hand and swaying on his feet. Shaw was staggering around on the dance floor all on his own unsuccessfully trying to achieve a deeply embarrassing version of The Twist and Spender was nowhere to be seen. Once Lucy had persuaded Alan and Shaw to leave, and this took some time as they weren't at all pleased, they eventually found Spender lying outside on a bench, asleep.

They all somehow got into the car. Alan fell into the driver's seat and immediately his head smacked forward onto the steering wheel. The two in the back seat were lolling around and mumbling.

Lucy was furious. What was she to do? She wanted to go home – now! She could drive. She had a driver's licence but she had only ever driven Mum's Morris Minor. Well, she wasn't going to stay here but she didn't have enough money for a taxi. She was so furious with Alan she wanted to punish him. She was still staying at home because of her job. Her parents and her siblings had already moved to the family beach house which was at least a two-hour drive away. Suddenly a moment of madness hit her. She would go there! Insane, but she'd show them.

It was a challenge shoving Alan over into the passenger seat but eventually she managed with one gigantic final push. He slowly rolled over so that his left his cheek was squashed against the side window. He groaned but didn't stir.

Lucy hopped into the driver's seat and started the car. It growled and whined and bounced every time she turned the key, finally letting out a metallic screech and settling into a reluctant sounding chug. Grinding the cranky old gear stick into first and edging out of the car park, tentatively practicing gear changes, Lucy finally felt she had the knack. She edged the Austin out onto the main road and set off for the beach feeling nervy and a bit sick.

The drive was a nightmare. Lucy was relieved there was a full moon as the headlights on the dinky little car were so dim that once she was off the sealed roads of the city and on the peninsular, juddering along the corrugated dirt roads in pitch dark was terrifying. She was so tense she felt she had lockjaw. Her shoulders and back were hurting because she was gripping the steering wheel so tightly with her nose almost touching the windscreen. What if they broke down?

Slowly, slowly they rattled along. Fortunately the dusty road with all its twists and turns was familiar and each time they passed one of the beaches she recognised, she knew they were making progress. Ah! There was the old country church on the hill overlooking their bay. Nearly there!

With less than a mile or so to go Lucy slowed down to a crawl, looking for an entrance to a field that had no vista or any buildings in sight. She found one. She drove in and parked the baby Austin right into the middle.

Getting out of the car, Lucy's legs almost gave way. She peered inside, found her purse and spied two unopened bottles of wine rolling around on the floor. She took those too and, leaving the driver's side door wide open, set off walking.

Daylight.

Crichton, Shaw and Spender gradually stirred. With headaches, sore necks and boozy eyes they raised their heads. They peered out the dust-caked windows. The scene was blurred.

'What the shit! Where the bloody hell are we?'

A PICNIC

'Get in the car.'

'But I can't find my big shovel.'

'Never mind. Dad's out there with the motor running.'

'But...but I **need** it.' Christo's face becomes red with frustration.

'What if the sand is 'xtremely hard and I have to dig a channel? Anna's dopey bucket and spade just won't do the job!'

Christo is already forming complicated plans for an awesome fort and as he had been given a real grownup shovel for Christmas – sized down admittedly – he isn't going to miss out on showing it off to all the other kids who'll be joining them for the beach picnic. Anna's plastic tools (after all she is only four) would be far too humiliating. Christo, recently turned seven, now has an inflated opinion about his superiority over his sister.

'*Get in the car Christopher.*' Christo gets in.

Relenting, Lucy runs through to the other side of the house and scoots down into the garden. There it is, the shovel, leaning with an abandoned air against a tree. She grabs it, runs back and throws it into the boot amongst all the other beachy clobber and hops into the passenger seat.

'All set?'

'Yes Dad – let's **GO!**'

Their house girl Lomani runs out onto the road laughing and waving them off.

'Bye Chriseeee. Bye Annaaaa. Bye Marama. Bye Sir!'

Two little blond heads squeeze out the back windows excitedly waving.

'Bye Mani'. See you tonight! Moce, Moce!'

In her bright red sulu Lomani stands out in the middle of the road laughing and waving as if life's big joke will never end.

They drive through the little residential compound with its houses nestling behind vivid tropical gardens, out onto the main road, past Natali's aromatic General Store with the usual assortment of locals in their brightly coloured sulus or saris sitting patiently lined up along the concrete terrace with their legs hanging over the edge, some dozing, waiting for the bus.

'Hey Man! What time is the bus due eh?'

'Three o'clock boss'.

'Is that three o'clock or three o'clock sharp?'

In the 1960s, according to Fiji Time, 'three o'clock sharp' means with luck the bus might turn up within fifteen minutes early or late. 'Three o'clock' is totally in the lap of the Fijian Gods or the weather, or the mechanical condition of the bus at the time, or the fact that the driver didn't bother to turn up at all. In the Colonial sixties it's a relaxed little world – Fiji.

***

Now they are on the juddery unsealed main road. A white cloud of coral dust trails behind them. Lucy in the front passenger seat moves her feet a little. As usual the car air conditioner is leaking despite the fact that Richard keeps reassuring her that he'll get it fixed. They are on their way to meet a group of other families to explore, according to their friend Malcolm McDonald, a fabulous newly discovered beach with amazing surf and sand.

Excited and full of optimism about the day ahead the children sing songs, play "I Spy" and speculate about all the adventurous things they will do when they arrive.

It takes some time to find the exit that leads off the main road and once on it they head off for about two miles towards the coast on an uncomfortably bumpy track that cuts through a sugar cane planation. Eventually they flush out onto the sand and there is the sea. The two-mile long beach is indeed fantastic, the land behind it being heavily wooded in some places. Stretching out of sight in both directions the sand is pale and untouched, backed by grassy dunes. Surf comes rolling towards them – luscious white foam as the waves slide along the shore. Beyond the sea is wonderfully blue.

They park alongside the gaggle of cars already arrived. Families are tumbling out with armfuls of beach gear. Children are running and jumping and rolling down the soft slippery sand dunes and onto the beach. Christo follows them and takes charge. He has an attentive audience. He, being the eldest, has a rapt group of admirers. He is their hero – the planner of exciting projects. Little kids of varying shapes and sizes gather as he outlines his architectural plans. They cluster around him – the boys with their arms folded across their bony bare chests and the girls together in their own group, giggling, snapping the legs of their elastic swimsuits, nudging each other.

'Right!' says Christo. 'Have you got that? Okay. Let's go.' and the compliant contingent follow him down the beach onto the flat smooth sand, their colourful plastic buckets and spades swinging against their legs and occasionally being flung into the air by the boys.

The main reason for a first visit to this beach is the fact that it is a new adventure but also that it is remote and private. Malcolm has bought a new boat – an inflatable rubber affair. Immediately they arrive the construction of the boat commences. It really is rather a good boat once the men get it assembled. It has bellows to inflate it and once pumped up, seats are installed as well as oars and Malcolm has dug up a grimy old outboard motor from somewhere. Launching it through the surf proves to be rather dangerous but after several attempts and a lot of hooting and laughing from the audience on the beach, the four men are sailing happily around outside the breakers with their rods and have already caught a good-sized fish.

The beach party – mothers – set up a picnic spot, sorting out the food they have brought, planting huge shady umbrellas and eventually sitting down to watch the men chugging back and forth beyond the breakers, occasionally bestowing their audience with a cheery wave. The women lie on their beach towels, hands above their sunglasses to shield the sun's glare, sunhats pulled down low. They watch the breakers throwing their froth onto the smooth sand and then sliding backwards to be swallowed up by the ocean.

But their exclusive occupation of the beach is brief. A small group of local boys appear some distance away. They are all dark and skinny. They head for the shallows dragging a horse they are leading on a rope. It is a thin starved creature. With its sad head hanging down it is not putting up any resistance. One of the older boys has a whip with which he is repeatedly flogging the horse's emaciated flanks. He is laughing. The beach party are horrified and the children, abandoning their fort construction, scream and cry out – pointing

Lucy starts to run along the beach. Her vague plan is to demand possession of the whip. As she runs she waves frantically at the boat party who are still skimming along outside the breakers and just as Lucy approaches the group of boys, Paul Harriman, the local Chief of Police, over six foot tall and recognised for his occasional unorthodox manner of dealing with offenders, rears up out of a wave and is beside the horse with the whip in *his* hand, flailing it about as boys scatter in all directions. He pursues the boys right up the beach and into the forest, rousting them in Hindustani and finally locks the whip in his car. He then leads the poor horse out of the water where it is standing despondently, removes the rope and gives its hindquarters a gentle slap. It wanders off in the opposite direction, disappearing up into the trees.

The boating party return to the shore riding a huge wave which pitches them into the surf. Bodies, hats, sunglasses, rods and fish are tossed about with the boat eventually ending up marooned on the beach upside down. This lightens the mood somewhat so lunch is produced but immediately everyone has settled down to eat, a huge thunderstorm rolls in. So, after deflating the boat everyone hastily packs up and heads for home.

***

In the back of the car two little people are very subdued.

'I didn't like today. I think we should have taken that horse home.' Anna's voice is very soft and quavery. 'Yes...it would have been happy with us' she adds tentatively.

'Oh it certainly would' says Christo stoutly. 'It'd be up to me to make sure it had lots of carrots and apples so it would get fat and comfy and have lots of fun when we'd go out for rides.'

The little voice again.

'But where would it live when the hurricanes come? Where would it sleep?' Tears well up.

'With Mani – silly' replies Christo.

Even the usually compliant Anna can't swallow that suggestion. Lomani's bure at the back of the house is not that roomy.

'All it wants is for people to love it. Let's ask Mani when we get home if she knows any of the Fijian people who live in the village up behind that beach. Then they could find it and bring it to live with us.'

'Good plan'. Christo bestows Anna with an approving nod. 'Yes – Mani will know what to do.'

He yawns.

'Are we nearly home Dad?'

ARROWTOWN GOLD

They were planning a test run.

Henry had received a new bike for his thirteenth birthday and boy, was he telling everyone about it. It was a BMX and it was only to be used when they were staying at Arrowtown. In fact, it was going to live there permanently, stored in the rickety shed behind their holiday cottage. Back home in Christchurch he'd still have to make do with his Raleigh. Grace could hear him banging on and on about it in the kitchen to his holiday buddy Logan, between mouthfuls of cereal

'Across the river' Henry was saying. 'We can go up the road to the right. There's plenty of places up there suitable for dirt jumps.'

There was no reply from Logan. Grace could actually hear him munching his cornflakes from her bedroom because it was located right next to the kitchen.

'Yeah' Henry continued. 'And we'll pick up drinks and pies at the cakeshop on our way through town, right?'

'Hmm – okay.' Logan's reply was muffled. He obviously still hadn't finished his cornflakes. Grace could hear him slurping up the milk at the bottom of the bowl. She jumped off the bed, still in her PJ's, opened her door and said, 'Can I come too?'

'Definitely not a good idea' Henry's response was lordly. 'We're going up the steep side across the river. You wouldn't cope.'

This reply was no surprise to Grace so she just said very firmly, 'No problem. I'm going to go up the left side. It's easier and prettier.'

'How do you know? You've never been up there.'

Grace didn't dignify that rebuff with any reaction at all. She just closed the door, flopped back onto her bed and gave serious consideration as to what to wear.

'Crap. What a drag' she heard Henry say.

***

It was a glorious day, cycling along towards the town's main street – past the playing fields and then under the avenue of magnificent lime trees, showing off their fresh Spring green. Past the white library that had once been a nineteenth century cottage. Past the solid square Georgian bank building, now painted in fashionable grey and the timber History Museum next door where Grace and Henry would often go down into the old cellars to see dioramas of life during the gold rush.

The main street, shining in the morning sun, was lined with quaint old timber buildings, all painted white, once miners' cottages, now converted into trendy boutiques and cafes attracting tourists.

Their snacks stowed in their backpacks the cyclists whizzed down the hill through the carparks, past the primitive shacks in the Chinese Village, now restored for tourists to poke their heads into and study the information boards relating the history of the area.

Down on the flat land the river flowed along – shallow, busy, crystal clear – stroking its bed of white arterial stones.

Over the arched bridge they sped, the tyres of the bikes juddering on the wooden planks. Once on the path on the other side the boys stopped. The mountain loomed above them. By noon it would start to throw its shadow down over the town as the sun moved its way West.

Grace, when she reached the end of the bridge, didn't stop. She sailed serenely left onto the path. The boys yelled

'Hey! We're going right y'know'.

Grace airily waved an arm and cycled on. The two boys hesitated for a moment or two, watching her and then Henry yelled out 'Okay – please yourself – bye!' and the two of them set off up the wide gravel track and disappeared around the side of the mountain.

Grace rode along beside the river. On her left on the opposite bank, people, mainly children, were crouching down with hired mesh bowls, sifting the silt on the riverbed, panning for arterial gold. It was a tourist thing. Grace and Henry used to take Mum's sieve down there when they were little and only once, in all the years of school hols, did they collect a miniscule lump of the arterial gold. She peddled on.

The path wasn't gravelled – just a nice firm earth surface with grass patches here and there. Eventually it took a wide sweep to the right at the base of the mountain, narrowing and immediately beginning to climb. The river, flowing from its source high up, was a fast-moving narrow stream, deep in places between sturdy banks decorated with ferns and other water loving plants. The path, just a track now, grew steadily steeper and narrower with windy bits and, in places, steps formed naturally in the landscape.

Grace was walking by now, wheeling her bike and humping it up over the steep bits. Miniature waterfalls were appearing. She came to a primitive bridge – just some sturdy logs that had been placed across the stream. She hesitated, doubtful. Should she go on? She looked upwards. The gorgeous rainforest soared above her decorated with tree ferns. Birds called, so clear and bell like with the hint of an echo. Everything smelt woody with the occasional acrid whiff of possum.

'I'd better be sensible and go back' she thought and then, somewhere above her she heard the sound of... what? Something was banging, metal upon metal. She wheeled her bike off the track and shoved it into a thick clump of ferns where it couldn't be seen, wobbled across the mossy logs and continued to climb.

It was steep and slippery in places and every now and then she stopped and had a rest, sitting on a fallen branch or a rock. The noise was getting closer so she took a good swig of water from the bottle in her backpack and forged on.

The forest canopy started to thin and eventually she rounded a bend and was confronted by an open field covered in pale scruffy grasses, illuminated in bright sunlight. She was standing at the beginning of a dirt road, completely straight, rising up and disappearing over a mound.

She walked on and over the top and there before her lay two rows of buildings divided by what appeared to be a main street. There were no people to be seen, just a horse tethered to a porch railing. The ringing noise which appeared to come from the right side of the street seemed really close now so she headed towards it.

Then suddenly, before she reached it, a woman stepped out of a cottage to her left. She was dressed in a long brown full-length gown. It appeared to be made of a heavy fabric with a very full skirt, tight at the waist, buttoned to the neck and long sleeves that puffed out towards her wrists. Her hair was drawn neatly into a tight bun at the back of her head with a very straight parting down the middle. Her face was full with hard little brown eyes.

'Wot 'r' y'doin'? she asked. Her accent was strange. 'Who 'r' you? Where've you come from?'

Grace took a couple of steps back and said, 'Oh, ah – I'm just taking a walk. Exploring...' She hesitated. The woman continued to stare at her so she ploughed on.

'I'm from Arrowtown – y'know – down the bottom of the hill.'

'There aren't no town down there.' The woman hesitated 'Missie...? She examined Grace's shirt and jeans and sneakers and continued, 'Y're a girl aren't ya? How old 'r ya?

Puzzled, Grace replied, 'Yes, that's right. I'm eleven.'

The woman eyed her up and down again, shrugged her shoulders and to Grace's surprise said, 'You'd be wanting a cup o' tea then?'

'Yes...please.' Grace was flummoxed but intrigued. The woman turned abruptly and led the way into the cottage.

It was made of raw timber – unpainted with a little roofed open porch along the front. Inside the walls were unlined. The floor was stone, very uneven. One room appeared to occupy the entire building with an iron stove, a simple board table and chairs at one end and at the other two beds with iron bedheads. Everything was very neat and organised. Outside, somewhere at the back, Grace could hear the contented clucking of chooks.

The woman pulled two metal mugs off hooks on the wall and put them on the table then she went to the stove where a huge kettle was already boiling and tipped the hot water into a metal teapot, spooning in several serves of tea leaves.

'Sit down girl' she said with her back to Grace. She opened a rustic cupboard and brought out a tin, removed the lid and turning, offered it to Grace. 'Will y'have a biscuit?'

'Thank you.' Grace took one and bit into it. It was grainy and only slightly sweet.

'It's very nice' she said and the woman smiled.

'I like your house too.' Grace continued, looking around. 'Very cosy'.

'Ay' the woman replied. 'It keeps us dry and warm in winter. Seamus – he built it and made the beds and furniture. He's across the street' she added, pointing.

'Is that the banging noise I can hear?'

'Ay... he's the blacksmith.' The woman nodded. 'Would ya loik t'see?'

'Oh yes please.' Grace hesitated and then said 'But I don't know your name.'

'I be Maura Donovan'.

'I'm Grace O'Connell!'

'So you be Irish!' Maura's stern expression brightened. 'You be from Country Kerry!'

'Well, no. We're from Christchurch actually.'

The woman didn't seem to relate to that piece of information at all and instead, stood up and said, 'Come along girlie.' leading Grace out the door. They crossed the street. The clanging and banging had stopped. Maura entered the building, the exterior of which appeared to be made of mud bricks. Grace followed her in.

'Look what I've found Seamus.'

The Smithy had a flagged floor made of individually shaped stones. There was a huge fireplace with a roaring fire and in front of it a man stood before an anvil with a horseshoe lying on it together with a heavy metal hammer.

Seamus stared at Grace, his hand on one hip, the other resting on the anvil. He looked her up and down as if he was assessing her. He grunted. He was a lean bony man but his arms in their rolled-up shirt sleeves were muscled. He wore a long leather apron with straps over his shoulders. His face was weathered, his brown hair cut short, his moustache was neatly trimmed.

'It's a girl' Maura said.

The man seemed to take more interest, studying Grace intently.

'How old 'r ya?' he growled.

'Hi Mr Donovan, I'm eleven.' Grace felt very uneasy – anxious actually. This was becoming very strange and just as she started to say, 'Well, I think I'd better be going now. My parents will be wondering...' two boys came bursting through the door – talking at once.

'Teacher sent us for eggs'

They looked like twins, perhaps around eight years' old. They were wearing tight knickerbocker pants to their knees above stout boots and handknitted socks. They had on rough jackets in a man's style and tight collared shirts, waistcoats and bow ties. On their heads were cloth caps, baker boy style with leather peaks.

'Foine' Maura said. 'I'll fetch some.' She turned and left the smithy.

The boys followed her so Grace, relieved to escape the strange atmosphere in the forge, tagged along. She hung around outside the house thinking that this would be a good time to make a getaway. She looked up at the sun and estimated it was around midday. But before she could skedaddle the boys came tumbling out of the cottage and one said, 'Me Ma, she says you should come wiv us.'

'Well – that's very nice of her but I really have to go...

The boy who had spoken grabbed her hand and said, 'No, Ma, she says you need to see the town' and he started to tow Grace along the dusty dirt road

'I'm Liam and me bruvver', he's Ronan.'

Reluctant but intrigued, Grace complied.

As they walked along she looked left and right at simple little houses interspersed with primitive commercial buildings, only really distinguishable by their signs. There was a bank, a Chinese laundry, a shop with tools and hardware, a lawyer's office, a General Store and more than one pub, all with signs advertising 'Rooms for Rent.' There was not one person to be seen. It was all so puzzling.

The boys turned left and guided Grace down a narrow lane at the end of which was the schoolhouse – a long whitewashed building with a drystone wall along the front. Clusters of children were sitting on top of the wall or standing in front of it, as if they were posing for a photograph. The boys were dressed the same as her companions and the girls all wore flouncy white pinafores over ankle length full dresses. They all had long hair. They all stared.

Liam said 'Wait here' and he and Ronan ran up the path and in the door. Within a minute they were back again which was a relief to Grace as she was still standing where they had left her, her audience looking at her with fixed stares and saying not one word.

'Cm along Miss' Liam said, taking her hand again and towing her. They walked back along the lane and turned left. This worried Grace because they should have turned right to return to the forge.

The main street stretched ahead but there seemed to be no end to it. Eventually there were no more buildings but they kept on walking and then abruptly the street ended and they were standing at the top of a sheer cliff. Down below was a rushing river, tumbling and foaming over rocks. On the far side a mountain rose up with steep sides and clustered all over them were lots of men working around diggings. Scattered timber structures were installed randomly, teetering on the hillside. Sounds of picks could be heard faintly in the distance but the river was mostly drowning out any sound other than its noisy course down through the gorge. To Grace's left she could see a fairly substantial timber bridge. A horse and dray were moving slowly across it guided by a number of men, all in rough clothing.

'What is this?' Grace exclaimed.

'They's The Claims.'

'Aye' Ronan said, nodding his head wisely. It was the first time he had spoken.

'Claims?' Grace asked.

'Aye. They's pitches claimed by the gold diggers. The river – tha' be The Shotover. Too dangerous t' pan furr arterial gold. D'ya want t' go down? Track be over there.'

Liam pointed. Ronan did too

Grace's anxiety was beginning to well up and make her face burn. She turned and said, 'Well – thanks a lot. That's been really interesting but I've got to go home now.'

She started to walk back along the road. She wanted to run but she sensed this might not be wise so she just forged on in a resolute manner, taking long strides. The boys, taken by surprise, in no time were walking alongside her.

Liam said, 'No – not home. This be your home. Ma and Da need a girl in the family. They be tryin' fur a girl fur years.'

Grace, terrified, began to run. She reached the first of the buildings and suddenly they all rose up on either side of her, floating and moving benignly above her as if they were balloons in a slight breeze.

She ran and ran but the street wouldn't end. It looked exactly the same as it did back where they looked over at the diggings. She felt she was on a treadmill, running in one place. She shed her backpack so she could go faster. She was crying. She was so full of fear she felt she was going mad.

And then, a building landed right in front of her, blocking her way. Seamus was standing leaning against the doorpost, his arms folded. He was grinning - leering. Grace screamed

'No! No! No!...'

***

'Grace! Grace! Darling! Wake up! What on earth are you doing in bed? The boys set off ages ago.'

Mum was standing over her. The sun was shining in through the window, bathing her bed with heat.

'You've had a nightmare' Mum said, stroking her hair back from her face. 'You're all sweaty! No wonder... the sun.' She pulled down the blind.

Grace sat up, sobbing. 'Oh Mum. That was so horrible. I was terrified. I'm never going into the History Museum ever again in my entire life!'

Her mother laughed and hugged her. 'Dreams fade.'

FROM THIS DAY FORWARD

'She's a bit of a cold fish.' Priscilla's father, Mr Vance, settled back in his armchair and regarded Ryland with a challenging expression.

'Despite the fact that she's so pretty' he added, as if it was an afterthought.

'She's a stayer though. Reliable. Never gives up on anything. Always gives it her best shot. Has never caused us any concerns.'

He nodded, appearing to give confirmation of his remarks to something outside the window.

Ryland shifted uncomfortably in his new black shiny shoes. He was still standing up as, so far, Cilla's father hadn't offered him a chair.

'Sit down son.' Mr Vance instructed, waving his half-smoked cigarette vaguely towards the other armchair in the room. Ryland sat – edge of the chair, back straight, knees together. Crikey! This was painful. When would it be over?

'SO' said Mr Vance extremely forcefully as if he was concluding a board meeting.

'I agree to your proposal. You've handled it very honourably son and I'm sure you'll be an excellent husband to my daughter and support and take care of her in every way.

'Thank you Sir.'

Ryland didn't know whether he should stand up and leave but suddenly his inherent feeling of self-worth took control and he shifted his long body comfortably back into the armchair and smiled at his future father-in-law.

'Thanks' he said, as if Cilla's father had just handed him a stein of beer. *'Establish an equal footing.'* His inner voice whispered. *'Don't give him the upper hand.'* Cyril Vance had quite a reputation at the Yacht Squadron for being somewhat overbearing.

'Well – off you go.' Mr Vance waved his newly lit cigarette in a dismissive manner. 'Better go out and give our little girl the good news.'

***

Cilla sat on the garden swing, the extravagantly full skirt of her fifties dress overflowing on either side of the chains. Her blond hair barely stirred as she gently pushed on the grass with the pointed toes on her pretty little pumps – pink to match the flowers on her dress – and began to swing slowly back and forth.

How did she feel? Well, nothing much really. Good old lanky Ryland with his oversized ears and that yucky soft fluffy hair sticking out above his lobes, was inside talking to Dad. Oh well – she knew he'd say yes. Ryland was a catch. The Hilliers were influential. They were rich - Eastern Suburbs Establishment. The engagement would be bandied about amongst the Dolly Levi's of the social set as a good match.

She did a quick calculation. It was still May. Hopefully the wedding could be before the 1954 summer was over. If it seemed rather rushed she could counter that by pointing out that it would far better be as soon as possible while the weather would still be warm. She could tell a lie and say she couldn't bear to think that she and Ryland couldn't be together until next year.

Anxiety welling up, she continued to float back and forth, assuring herself that she could charm Dad into getting her way. Mummy might be a bit more of a challenge because of all the elaborate wedding arrangements that she would deem essential to impress their friends. Cilla, however, was determined.

***

Ross. She must stop herself agonising about Ross. After he dumped her during that humiliating lunch at their fave café, The Cosy Nook, in tears she'd forced herself to go back to the office where she sat in front of her typewriter in utter misery.

She loved Ross. She was mad about him. She knew it was her own fault. She loved him so much she'd become jealous and they'd had a really big argument after the Bank of NZ Ball because he had danced with Sheila Pocock three times.

This wasn't the first time she'd been a pain and had nagged on at him about Sheila. He kept on patiently reassuring her that they were just old friends and that he was in love with her, Cilla, but she still couldn't help herself. She was violently jealous.

She tried to reassure herself that they would marry. He seemed so keen on her. Whenever they'd be going on a date and he arrived to pick her up and was in the living room with her parents she'd wait in her room and then make an entrance and he'd look at her and pretend to swoon and make a funny sucking noise through his teeth as if he was going to eat something delicious.

Mummy and Daddy thought he was hilarious and they'd laugh their heads off – every time. And she fancied him dreadfully. She'd get tingles up her spine when she even thought about him and would relish that feeling during their dates and the knowledge that once they were in the car he'd drive to a quiet place and they'd neck and it was lovely. So romantic.

The day he broke up with her, as usual she caught the bus home. She ran straight into the kitchen, bursting into tears and throwing herself face down on the linoleum floor. Mum just continued to stand at the sink peeling potatoes. Later, after Cilla had finished her paroxysm of weeping (she was flat on her face on her bed by now) Mummy had come in and put her arms around her and held her while Cilla wept on her shoulder.

'Never mind darling' said Mum. 'There'll be lots of others.'

How could she say that! She didn't want 'Others'. Ross was the only man for her.

She didn't feel like that with Ryland. She felt nothing actually. She didn't fancy him at all. But she had to marry someone.

That one night after the barn dance, well, Ross had become so passionate they'd gone all the way in the back seat of the Morris Minor. It was a bit of a shock, all that fumbling around in such a confined space. But despite that, she still adored him and now the tingly feeling was even stronger.

And then, a few weeks after that she was late. She didn't tell a soul – just went and saw a doctor way over on the North Shore and was told she was pregnant. And then, after that dreadful news and behaving so badly at the ball, Ross dumped her. She was absolutely devastated. She knew she could never tell him. She would never tell anyone.

And now here came Ryland, striding down through the garden with his suit jacket flapping and a goofy grin on his face. Oh God!...

She hopped off the swing, smiling, and then it was as if she was in one continuous ballet movement as Ryland was picking her up and swinging her around and around as if it would be forever and ever.

THE LITTLE BLACK BACH

The room is white – all white except for a black iron bedstead. What day is it? Monday. Good. Not too many more days to go including New Year's Eve. Ugh … get that over and done with. She lies on her back, her arms behind her head and studies the suffused sunlight as it moves about the room.

If she were to open the creamy linen curtains a headland and valley would be revealed laden with New Zealand native bush – palm trees, pungas, pine trees, nestling houses and beyond, an unbelievably blue sea. And in the foreground a silvery grey wooden deck with a black railing, a dense young lemon tree with tiny green ovals forming and incongruously, a green plastic washing line stretching across the view with a merry little red wire bucket full of multi-coloured pegs like a perching basket of lollies.

At night the south-westerly wind is gone leaving just a gentle breeze and the leaves of the flax outside her window stroke and flap softly like fabric. Little creatures move in the leaf litter, probably the rabbit she spied polishing off the vegetable peelings she had tossed into the garden before dinner. A morepork sends out its repetitive two-tone night call. During the day a tui visits a big tree. Its call is delightful and unique with its vocal bell-like acrobatics. The tree is also visited by a wood pigeon – large, fat with impeccable markings clearly defined in jade green and white. Its wing beats flap wonderfully, loudly. One afternoon five vivid little Australian rosellas turn up and are chased off by the tui.

She loves the island. It is beautiful and familiar territory with its complex coastline replete with little bays, long soft beaches and creamy cliffs decorated with pohutukawa trees wearing their red summer flowers. Its lush foliage indicates plentiful rainfall, a painful contrast to all she has left at home. 'Home' – strange that she is calling Australia home. Even though three quarters of her life has been lived in other places in the world, she still regards New Zealand as Home.

But it is 2019 and Australia is on fire and that's where her house is – where she lives. Since she arrived she has been counting the days to her return. The TV news shows horrifying scenes of the fires so that some evenings she can't watch. Despite her fear she wants to be at home to protect her house which is ridiculous – one small person with a hose confronting those infernos. Her stomach permanently aches with anxiety.

The house, The Little Black Bach, is sweet – ideal for the two of them, her and her widowed friend. It rambles about and is full of light and the owner's possessions. Artworks, books, clusters of decorative pieces artfully arranged, some wearing ethereal cobwebs, create a feeling of hominess. She studies the owner's snapshot on the fridge. A big woman – the Taj Mahal is in the background.

She's bored. It would be preferable to be bored in her own home despite the smoke and fear. There are things to do there – to keep her occupied. Here she reads during the day and late into the night devouring four books in one week. Her family, holidaying in Bali, phone her. It's not her scene, Bali, even though she remembers its beauty when she visited it long ago before it became a tourist destination.

So here she is, keeping her friend company. Not good company it's turned out. They haven't spent serious time together for many years. Their friendship stretches back to school days. But now their conversations are awkward, desultory. She feels she bores her friend who stares at her with a strange expression when she is stating an opinion. She often feels inferior intellectually, that her friend disapproves, that she is assessing her in some negative way, that she is impatient with her and condescending. They skirt around debatable subjects to avoid conflict and consequently their exchanges are vapid. Sometimes a gentle rebuke. Often an opposing opinion hinted at but never fully expressed. Just 'Yes, well.....' and that superior dismissal. It's depressing and humiliating. Once, sometime ago in another place she remembered challenging her. 'Stop criticising me so often'. The stare...... 'Honestly, you really are the pits' she had said and walked away.

Her friend forces her out. 'Come for a walk.' Problem. Too many hills and traffic on narrow winding roads. Up the hill they plod. The road twists through native bush and impressive houses perch precariously on the steep hillsides. At the top a nice flat road and views. Oh the views! A bus full of tourists turns up to spoil the moment so they go home.

One afternoon her friend says 'I think we should try the beach at the bottom of the hill. We'll drive down – it's too steep to be walking back up again'.

The bay is small – intimate. It's like a big round swimming pool held within the protective folds of two deep cliffs. A natural barrier of dark rocks straggles across the exit to the sea with a narrow gap for a very small craft to squeeze through. The whole bay is rocky with very little sand so they teeter over the stony surface to a shady spot. They settle down to the old familiar pastime of beach watching.

People sit, swim, call out, laugh, splash or bob about. Some swim purposefully, others just stand chatting, waist deep, swirling their arms around. It's a little circular world of freedom and pleasure. The sun shines. The sea is blue. The smell is salty. Faded islands float in the far distance. Big and small yachts out beyond the breakwater appear and disappear behind the protective cliffs as if passing on and off a stage.

Inside the sheltered pool, amongst the vivid colours of countless kayaks, young children and teenagers paddle around, mill about, rocking the colourful crafts, laughing, squealing, having fun. A mother, a voluptuous Polynesian woman in a vivid bathing suit, wades waist deep beside a yellow kayak, teaching a little boy how to use the paddle. Her voice carries to all corners of the natural auditorium.

'Reverse now! No! Use the other end of the paddle. That's it – very good. Whoops! Mind the rocks!'

A group of young men wearing black wetsuits and carrying flippers and snorkels skirt around the edge of the bay. They step gingerly avoiding the crusty oysters on the rocks and disappear around the headland. They reappear – sleek sliding black vessels with vertical funnels cruising around the breakwater.

The tiniest toddler in a pink frilly bathing suit and hat stands motionless between her mother's legs, on the very edge of the water, watching her feet as the little lapping waves creep up and stroke them. She holds out her fat little arms and flaps her hands up and down when a wave comes. She watches and watches.

Packing up she says 'I enjoyed that much more than going to the big sandy beaches' and her friend agrees so they return the next day.

***

'Oh my god! That view! I had no idea…!'

She is walking right through and out of another friend's island house, onto the terrace. This bach is on a cliff. The sea spreads out to the left, to the right and before her to eternity. The blue is intense – the ocean, the sky, the agapanthus in the foreground clustering along the edge of the deck. She feels as if she is overlooking the entire world. So very far below lies the beach – long and cream and smooth – the waves breaking and receding leaving beautiful fluid abstract patterns on the unblemished sand. Foreshortened figures stroll along the water's edge accompanied by their squat shadows or set off swimming out into the cobalt water. She stands there in wonder. Her friend looks pleased. They have talked about the house often during the years they have known each other, but this is the first time she has seen it. They spend several days together, visiting art galleries and vineyards and restaurants. There is a substantial cultural presence on the island – artists and writers. She is glad she has spent time with this friend.

***

They are in the queue for the vehicular ferry. She feels almost happy – relaxed and relieved that she is escaping the island and the sense of entrapment. She also feels guilty that this time she has not enjoyed that beautiful place. There are only three more days to go before she flies home.

166

The orange ferry arrives with exemplary efficiency and fluoro jacketed men and women conduct the vehicles on and off simultaneously. The system is like a big immaculately organised round-about. Finally an enormous semi-trailer is skilfully loaded. No time is wasted. They're off. The ferry shudders slightly then slides smoothly away from the wharf. People immediately leave their cars to go to the upper deck where they will sit and drink coffee, eat salty crisps and soggy chips. The wind is cold once the ferry moves out of the bay but most of the passengers are wearing scanty clothing, impervious to the chill. She opens the car window to enjoy the cool air. The smell of diesel floats in. A breakwater slides past. Headlands with their houses placed amongst the bushland watch benignly. They pass boats bobbing on their anchors and yachts slope by leaning over in the wind. The water is choppy in the channel but the heavy ferry slices through cleanly with no pitching. The eastern suburbs of the city outskirts come steadily closer. Extravagant houses are scattered along the cliffs. They have arrived.

***

The plane carries her smoothly into Sydney and she manoeuvres efficiently through the arrivals hall despite the mass of passengers and eventually flushes out of the terminal, up into the adjacent car park and is soon in her car, bowling homewards between a crisp drought-burnt countryside. Far in the distance she can see an ominous brown sky. Charred trunks of a million eucalypts line the highway as, in trepidation, she travels the last thirty kilometres. The smell of smoke invades the sealed interior of the car. She passes the tragedy of an utterly devastated village – every house blackened and burnt with the odd piece of brickwork still vertical – a chimney, a wall. She drives up onto the plateau. The little towns are still there, intact, just as she had left them but enveloped in smoke haze.

She drives up her hill beside the soaring cypress hedge that shields her property from the road, turns in through the gates and there are all the old trees and the hedges and the winding driveway and a glimpse of the house beyond them. Around the last bend, there it is, safe! with its silver iron roof, its verandahs, the main garden sloping away down through the oaks and elms and birches.

She opens the car door and a strong smell of smoke assails her. The fires are still threateningly near – to the south, the west, the north. She turns the key in the front door. The usual stuffy atmosphere of an old, uninhabited house has been permeated by the smell of smoke. She inhales – savouring it.

Yes. Home...

THE CHILDREN'S ISLAND

Christo and Anna loved going to the island. Well – it was such a little island and so flat that it was really only an atoll. One could walk around it in about 15 minutes. In the middle there were a few palm trees and at the back of the pale sandy beach the occasional dune. There were some flat smooth rocks in places at the water's edge and occasionally a big turtle would be discovered just floating in the rhythm of the gentle waves that lapped the shore.

With their mother and father, Christo and Anna and all the other mums and dads and their little children would arrive in the motorboat laden up with lunches, drinks, towels, suntan lotion, hats, flippers, goggles, beach balls, cricket gear – all manner of beachy paraphernalia. Sometimes a little sailing dingy would be brought along as well.

All the children, however small, could swim pretty well and would spend most of the time in the water – that is if they weren't sailing back and forth in one of the boats supervised by one of the dads or doing sporty things on the beach or playing pirates or building forts and castles. Very occasionally there would be a minor mishap like the day Anna stood on a sea cucumber and it squirted horrible white sticky stuff around her ankle. It didn't sting and she was admirably stoic about it. However, if anyone spotted a *damdakalave*, everyone headed for the shore quick smart. These were sea snakes – a scary bright blue with black stripes and although venomous they were docile creatures and would never attack humans unless severely provoked. Even so, no risks were taken. It was wise to clear off when they were around.

At lunchtime all the food would be set out on a communal rustic table that the dads had built and then everyone would go and sit on the beach to eat. One day Christo was sitting up on a little dune and suddenly, right out from under his bottom and all around him, hundreds of baby turtles started to emerge from the sandy mound. They immediately began to scurry towards the water's edge and as the birds started circling, the children ran along beside the turtles scooping up as many as possible and rushing them into the water. They looked like hundreds of little green scarabs. There was an abandoned dingy on the beach with some bilge in the bottom and as the numbers of baby turtles increased the children couldn't keep up.

'Tip them into the dingy' Christo yelled – taking charge. 'Someone stand guard and we'll come back and rescue them later'. The excitement and urgency was intense with little bodies running back and forth with their small hands like cups trying to help the vulnerable tiny creatures to reach the uncertain safety of the sea.

It had been one very special day.

During the wet season in Fiji sometimes island days had to be called off because it was just too wet to bother but one particular day all the mums and dads decided to risk it and go. It turned out to be a good decision as the sky remained blue and clear and everyone was enjoying their usual routine including a lot of sunbathing by the young mothers in their brightly coloured bikinis.

Suddenly another boat was spotted approaching the island. This appearance caused all the children to stop whatever they were doing. It was the first time that strangers had ever dared to intrude on their private paradise. They all stood still and stared.

A man and woman arrived in a rowing boat and when they reached the shallows the woman hopped out, dragged the dingy a little way over the water's edge and laid a beach towel down on the firm sand. The man then got out of the boat, sat down on the towel, took off one of his legs, laid it on the towel and then went for a swim. This event was observed in open mouthed awe and utter silence by the young contingent. It was as if they were frozen in motion. From then on nothing could divert them. The speculation about what had happened to the man grew more and more gruesome. Finally, one of the dads herded them all into the motorboat to take them for a spin around the island. 'To try to take their minds off it' he said, but it didn't work. When they returned he said the discussion had continued on and on interminably and that Christo (a gory little critter in the Dad's opinion) had authoritatively announced

'Well I know all about it. Because I asked his mother and I happen to know there was blood and more blood – five dollars' worth'.

The children's island days continued but no future event ever surpassed The Day of the Missing Leg.

CHRISTMAS DAY

I go to bed at 11pm. I take my little anxiety pill and that gives me a calm six or seven hours of uninterrupted sleep. If I go to bed earlier, especially in the summer, then next morning I am awake far too early as it tends to be rather noisy at the crack of dawn, the kookaburras especially and in summer a migratory bird that sometimes calls throughout the night – a long haunting repetitive call. Apparently it is a Koel, a type of cuckoo from South East Asia that lays its egg in other birds' nests, tossing out their eggs or chicks. Nasty thing.

Taking the little pill also means my sleep is not interrupted by Them when They roam round my garden smoking cigarettes. I know this because I find stubs tossed onto the nature strip outside my front gate. They also get up into my roof. I've installed flood lights and cameras but all they record are possums eating my climbing roses. They, the Others, are very clever, very tricky. I've called the police often. They are always young (the police) and at first, when it started, they were cheerily reassuring and polite but gradually they became quite impatient with me and rude and now they don't even turn up when I call them.

Tonight, as I watch TV and wait for 11pm it is raining – the gentle steady rain that I love. I'm hoping it will continue in this way until I get into bed so I can listen to its rhythmic sound on my roof – consistent so that the gutters don't overflow but just the right amount to hear the water gurgling in the downpipes.

Yes, I go to bed at 11pm every night, just as the freight train comes by at the bottom of my hill. I like to hear it sliding along, sometimes quite loud if the wind is from the south, the wheels screeching at times, metal upon metal. And then it fades away as it continues its journey between the fields and the country towns to its destination. Tonight, when I went into the kitchen to rinse my teacup and saucer it was starting to get dark and through the trees I could see a row of lights running along the front fence of my neighbours' house. Christmas lights?

Is it Christmas already? These neighbours have children – three I think. I wouldn't know. I never see them. They have lived next door for about eighteen months now. Shortly after they had moved in, I met the husband Peter over the fence at the little gate between our properties - only because their young dog was barking at me. We had a nice long chat which he ended (did I sense with some relief?) by kindly telling me to contact them should I need help with anything, like changing a light bulb. He actually said that – 'changing a light bulb'. So I bought a card with the greeting 'Welcome to your new home' and wrote my contact details on it – mobile phone number, email and popped it in their letter box and I've never seen or heard from them since! Oh well ... no doubt they are very busy with three young children and both with jobs. They are quiet although they do seem to use a lot of heavy machinery on weekends. Buzz saws, mulchers, leaf blowers. That irritates me I admit.

I do miss Pat though. She was such a good neighbour. That is why we had the gate. She's moved to one of those retirement villages. The property became too big for her and the expenses became impractical. At our age you have to watch your spending because if you live too long you might have to start eating into Capital. I've always kept that in mind. Old Jolyon in Galsworthy's 'The Forsyte Saga' was a stickler for never touching Capital and managed to remain rich right up to his death. I'm a self-funded retiree. I'm not rich but I'm financially secure. I have managed to do quite nicely on the Stock Exchange. Just Blue Ribbon stocks mind.

Now I'm feeling very worried as my Accountant Bernard has advised me that he is retiring! Why? I'm really annoyed with him actually as he is surely still only in his late seventies! I don't know what I am going to do without him. He came and picked me up and drove me to meet another Accountant whom he recommended. I didn't like him at all. When we had our meeting I explained about Them and my concerns that They wanted to take my house from me and drive me out. He was extremely dismissive and changed the subject. Bernard never did that. He was very understanding. About my concerns. So since the meeting I've persistently called him asking him to continue to manage my financial affairs and the other day he finally said (did I sense a whiff of exasperation?) 'Oh, alright Beatrice. For a year or two more then'. He probably calculates I'm going to fall of the twig within that time. I'm 92.

Pat was always so understanding when I'd phone her up and tell her to come in urgently as I needed her advice. We'd go way down towards the back of the garden and sit on the old seat so They couldn't overhear us. She was always so sympathetic and concerned about my predicament and would make very practical and reassuring suggestions. On one occasion I told her I wanted to see a lawyer and she said 'But you have a lawyer – the one who has your Will' but I said I didn't feel he was supportive like Bernard my Accountant and was making no effort to solve my problems and that was why I wanted to see someone else.

Finally, after I had raised the subject numerous times she took me to *her* lawyer who was a very nice young man. We went in together and I started to tell him about my worries and anxieties and while I was starting to tell him all about Them, I caught him glancing at Pat and eventually, when I stopped for a moment to collect my thoughts he said 'Now Beatrice (I'd rather he called me Mrs Bassinger – he's so young. But everybody calls everyone by their first name these days it seems – doctors and policemen for example, all of whom look twenty-two or so). 'I'm going to ask Pat to leave us now' he continued 'as our discussions will be confidential of course'. And I said 'Of course' even though I knew that I had told Pat everything at some stage during all the years we had known each other. Anyway, I told him everything as well and he was very respectful and reassuring saying there was no way that anybody could take my house from me. He repeatedly kept asking me whether I definitely had a Will which I found quite insulting and even though I couldn't think of the name of the solicitor I was able to tell him where his rooms were located (my solicitor that is) and he said he was sure he could guess which practice it would be. He assured me that I didn't have anything to worry about at all so I felt quite comforted as he escorted me out to Reception where Pat was waiting for me.

I love my house and garden. I bought the property with my inheritance after my mother died – while I was still working for Malcolm. I was his bookkeeper managing his business and personal accounts. I must say he was doing very well financially at the time, until the divorce. His wife made sure she got pretty much everything including their house. Before that happened he had told me loved me and I certainly knew I had loved him for years so he came to live with me. He was a wonderful man – handsome and urbane. We were so happy. I'm not really Mrs Bassinger as we never married. I'm really Miss Beatrice Mason which would be a Ms these days.

So that's when They put in an appearance – his children – after Malcom died. He had cancer and was ill for a long time and I nursed him through it all. I was in such a state of grief after he had gone that my eyebrows and eyelashes fell out and then there was also the attack. I was in the supermarket car park, loading my groceries when this young man came up behind me and bashed me so hard on the back of my head that I toppled over into the boot! Some kind rescuer fished me out and got me on my feet but of course my handbag was gone. I became *seriously* ill after that episode and was in hospital for a while.

Now it's nearly thirty years since Malcolm died. I've never got over it really. That happiness with Malcolm came to me quite late – in my fifties. Up until then I would never have believed that I could have been so lucky and so content.

But now I'm getting quite annoyed about that young lawyer Pat took me to. I've never heard a word from him about how he is going to solve my worries. Mind you, I've never received a bill from him either. Well, that's not surprising as the people at the post office are always opening my mail. I'm continually confronting them about it and reporting them but of course they deny it. Perhaps he's waiting for me to ask him to draw up a new Will. I told Pat that I was annoyed and asked her to help me find a copy of my current one and we searched around in the safe in the spare bedroom for ages, hauling out screeds of folders and laying them out on the bed. I have no idea what is in them. Eventually Pat said 'Bea, I'm uncomfortable with this – truly' and started to stack the files back into the safe. So that was that, but I still feel very let down by her lawyer. Nobody seems willing to really help me resolve my worries.

Yes ... I really miss Pat. The only people I see since she has gone are the Meals on Wheels lady - nice but bossy. Talks on and on. And my cleaner, 'Mary Down the Middle'. I call her that privately because she's not thorough and always in a hurry. All she gives my house is "A lick and a promise" as Mother used to say.

Goodness! Is that my phone ringing? It is, but where is it? They come inside the house now and continually keep stealing things or moving them around and my mobile phone is always the first thing to go missing. I have to keep going to the telephone company to buy a new one and every time they sell me one it is more complicated than before. When Pat was still next door I would take each new phone in to her and she would sort it out for me. I cancelled my land line because They were listening to my calls.

'Hello.

(I found it.)

Hello?'

'Hello? **Hello!** Aunty Beatrice? Merry Christmas! It's Margaret. How are you? Are you alright? All on your own as usual on Christmas Day.'

Margaret is my niece – lovely girl. Lives somewhere in Victoria. Her mother was my favourite sister but she died a few years' ago. Margaret keeps in touch all the time. Lovely girl. She has several grandchildren – I can't remember how many and always has delightful stories to tell about the funny things they have said and done. I see her perhaps once a year when she and her husband Phil come and visit me. They have a caravan and go touring all the time. They've been everywhere in Australia but they make sure they include my neck of the woods on their itinerary as often as possible so they can pop in. They don't stay with me. They stay in the caravan park in town which, they say, having had so much experience with such places, is a very good one. Margaret knows all about my worries and is very reassuring when we talk about them. Lovely girl.

But I've been taking up too much time, nattering on. It's always nice to have a confidential chat, especially as apparently, according to Margaret, it's Christmas Day. It must be quite late as it's dark now and the lights are twinkling away along the fence next door. Well, they look a bit wobbly actually, the twinkling lights, as it's still raining. I'd better go and check all the deadlocks. What did I have for dinner? Did I have dinner? Never mind – a cup of tea and a biscuit will be fine and after that I'll be off to bed.

At 11 o'clock.

THE NOTEBOOK

Imogen was out of the car like a shot. Running, running along the path to the front door then – whoa! – she tripped on one of the steps and spreadeagled onto the verandah so that when Gran opened the door all she saw was something resembling a very colourful starfish with a lot of jumble scattered around it. Everyone laughed including Immy. Dad and her stepmother Penelope and Gran and Margo gathered her up and shoved all the bits and pieces back into her pretty pink carry bag and they all went inside.

At seven years' old Imogen absolutely loved her weekends at her grandmother house. The drive from Sydney would take ages and was pretty boring. She could get a least five princess drawings done on the way ready to show Margo as soon as she arrived. Dad would have cool driving music on as they sped along the highway which seemed to make the time go slightly faster. The view outside the window appeared as if they weren't moving at all. It was just gumtrees, gumtrees and more gumtrees. 'Eucalyptus' was the real name Pennie said. Immy wrote it down. 'Yucaliptis'. That could be a good name for one of her princesses.

As they got near to Gran's things got more interesting and she could feel that delicious excited tingling feeling in her tummy and up her back. First there would be the long steep hill and then the big curvy turn off the highway and as soon as she spotted the Bunnings store she knew it wouldn't be too much longer, that is, unless Pennie and Dad stopped to pick up a coffee in one of the towns. Why couldn't they wait until they got to Gran's place? She could never understand it. It was SO unnecessary.

Gran had a very old house and a magical garden. She also had everything Immy might think of for her creative work like coloured pencils, paints, textas, glue and loads of paper and cardboard from the office which was at the end of the house. She had masses of colourful scraps of fabrics, ribbons, buttons, beads, sequins – just everything. Imogen and Margo, who was her aunt, would completely take over the TV room known as The Den and the carpet would very soon be littered with so much stuff it was sometimes hard to find a piece of floor to walk on.

In the office there was also Immy's cupboard full of books and toys that stayed at Gran's. Amongst them, but not in the cupboard because it didn't fit, was the most beautiful fairy castle. It was every colour you would see in an ice cream parlour. You felt you could take a big bite out of it. In it lived dozens of princesses, princes, unicorns, horses – every lovely thing. It would be squeezed into the den and every night, before bedtime, Immy would set up some entertainment at the castle for the fairies who lived in Gran's garden. Usually it would be a ball or a party. Invitations would be written in a notebook inviting the Fairy Queen and all her entourage to come.

'Hello fairys there is a ball hapning tonight Do you want to come could you invite the eLf king the fairy Queen all the fairys and eLfs and all the unicorns and mermaids Dont forget the butter flys and birds give everyone a night off please write back love Imogen'

A pen would be placed beside the notebook and next morning Immy would be out of bed and straight into the den to see if there was a reply. There always was.

Margo was very artistic. She was a 'Designer'. She could draw the most amazingly exotic princesses for Immy who would colour them in and then they would both have a long discussion about what to call them. Once that was decided Immy would write the name beside the drawing and a detailed description of the personality of the princess. While they were doing this they would play DVD's – movies from 'The Forties' and 'The Fifties'. Margo had explained what that meant so she knew all about it. They loved the old musicals and knew all the songs.

Sometimes, in the evening when the grownups were having 'Drinks', Immy would put on an art exhibition. She would make a big sign 'Art Show on Tonight $2 each'. She'd sell quite a few princess paintings and put the takings into her big china pig money box. She liked making signs. There was one in the guest bathroom which read 'Hugs 50 cents but only if yuve got the money then ther free'.

In the garden Imogen and Margo would walk around to see which flowers were out. In winter camellias, winter roses, early snowdrops and sometimes a peeping violet and the first of the masses of daffodils to come. And then in spring there were so many different flowers it was hard to count except they were mainly pink, purple and white. In autumn they would do leaf raking and hunt for toadstools and when they found any Immy would know that the fairies were near. In fact, she knew that the fairies were watching them whatever time of year it was. It was very comforting.

Sunday after lunch it was time to leave. Bags were lined up in the hall and Gran would cruise around the house to check if anything had been forgotten. It nearly always had. She wouldn't find it until after they had left. Once all the hugging was over Gran and Margo would stand on the verandah and wave. Around the winding driveway the car would go, disappearing between the hedges where Immy could only see the top of Gran's and Margo's arms waving and she would get a big lump in her throat.

***

Imogen is now fourteen and staying at Rainey's. She is busy making dolls' clothes for her little cousins on Rainey's electric sewing machine. Hunting for some buttons in a drawer she finds a notebook with "Write Here" on the front cover and "Where are you?" on the back and inside letter after letter written over many years until she was too grown up to believe in fairies any more.

GRAY

The monochrome garden had a misty light. Was it mist? Was it smoke? It was as if the winter garden was displayed through a pale diaphanous veil. Vertical rays of white sunlight formed spotlights creating a vivid streak across the width of the mossy lawn at the far end of the garden, as if an artist had taken his brush and made a confident chartreuse swipe across a grey canvas. Behind it the untidy tangle of jasmine along the far boundary appeared black. The deciduous trees were a silhouette; not a skerrick of wind stirred the oaks and elms; every plant was absolutely still with even the dewdrops suspended. The dark green camellia leaves appeared black, lit with silver tops and the intricate tangled web of bare branches on the old hawthorn tree outside the bedroom window were the softest shades of ancient grey decorated with pale olive-green fluffy lichen.

A delightful territorial warble began. A pair of immaculate magpies strutted past looking fat and important as they fluffed up their feathers against the cold and stabbed the ground for worms.

The neighbours' tan and white terrier Splodge, on the loose as usual, came trotting purposefully across the lawn heading for home, every now and then stopping to sniff the ground for traces of fox or rabbit. He headed into the hedged woodland and squeezed his fat bottom with its upturned tail through the gap between the boundary gate and the fence.

Laura Gray stood as still as the windless garden. A whiff of melancholy hovered around her, touching her heart. Was it the visual moment? Was it more significant than that? She had no idea so she turned to routine things. She showered and dressed and walked out into the long hallway. Minkie the cat was sitting halfway down and greeted her with one of her comforting little 'mirrups'. She was a rescue – an oriental mix of the softest grey with a white belly and the most beautiful blue eyes. She was vocally responsive and generally replied when anyone spoke to her. She stood up, stretched, raised her tail and escorted Laura into the kitchen where Laura put the kettle on, noticing that it was warm which meant that Hugo must be up.

There he was – at the dining room table with the morning papers spread all around him, a cup of coffee at his elbow. Laura gave him a light kiss on the top of his head. 'Hmmm' he responded. He was stabbing aggressively with his forefingers on his laptop, no doubt writing some letter of objection to one of the newspapers. The cat sprang up onto the table, sat down and stared at the screen. 'Hello The Minks' said Hugo, receiving a comforting 'brrrp' in reply.

Hugo's shoulders were hunched over his task. With his glasses perched on the end of his nose he thrust his chin forward each time he paused to check the script. Laura felt a lurch of motherliness. He looked boyish and vulnerable. 'He's still an attractive man' she thought. Smooth skin, a good head of greying hair. Heavier than when she first met him in his fifties, but solid – not paunchy or flabby. In his mid-seventies as was she, he still attracted women. Laura's friends occasionally remarked that he was 'dishy' and that she was 'a lucky duck'.

'What's on today Hugo?'

'Oh, I don't know. Haven't made any plans. You?'

'It's Book Club this afternoon. I'd better go. I've read the book.'

Laura took her cup of tea back into the kitchen, replenished it and sat down at the island counter. Yes, she must go. It would be rude not to turn up as their numbers were dwindling at a frighteningly rapid pace. Twenty years was a long time. They would all have been in their fifties or early sixties when it was first formed – by invitation only. Laura did a quick calculation. She would have been fifty-four. They had limited the number to ten – now they were down to six. Sometimes they had to cancel altogether like the time Marcia phoned and said 'Book Club's off. Everyone's falling over.'

She went. The hostess for the month lived in a very socially accepted retirement village in one of the delightfully designed bungalows, all cosily squashed in amongst pretty gardens, immaculately clipped hedges and topiaried trees. Like most women in Laura's age group, where they should live in their old age was a subject that seemed to turn up far too often although statistics, according to the media, indicated that most elderly people remained in their own homes right up to the end. Several Book Club members, if they hadn't already died, had made the transition into retirement villages and Laura inwardly shuddered when one of them remarked 'No 37 is up for sale' which meant that the occupant had died or was now in aged care.

'No' Laura assured herself, thinking of her beloved house and garden. 'I'll stay where I am no matter what.'

But what about Hugo. What did he want? They never discussed anything of substance any more. They just seemed to exist in a calm removed sort of way, each in their own individual internal and external spaces. They'd teamed up over twenty years' ago. Hugo was divorced and Laura was already on her own having separated from her husband a year or two before. They'd met at a concert at the Sydney Opera House. Mutual friends introduced them. Initially no sparks but she did think him handsome and he had a lovely speaking voice, an attribute she always found attractive in men. They dated for a few months and then Hugo asked Laura whether she'd like to accompany him on an overseas business trip and that cemented the relationship. He kept his apartment in Sydney and she remained in her house in the Southern Highlands and they comfortably moved back and forth between the two. Life was good.

Book Club was enjoyable. Everyone liked the book and spent more time than usual discussing its merits and that of the author's previous publications. They drank tea and complimented the hostess on her homemade cake. Afterwards Laura dropped eighty-one year old Patricia off at her very expensive residential complex with its immaculate gardens complete with a fountain, indoor swimming pool and stylish rooms. She helped Patricia out of the car, organised her walker and escorted her into the foyer where she was greeted by a bright faced girl who waved Laura off with a cheery thank you. Laura called out 'Bye Pat – see you next month' but Pat didn't hear her as she was chatting to the girl as she hobbled her way painfully along the corridor to her bed sitting room.

'Thank heavens' Laura said out loud as she drove home. 'Let me be a lucky one and stay in my own home.'

Driving through the dusk a warm feeling of contentment swept over her. She had a casserole in the fridge which only needed heating up and Hugo would pour her a gin and tonic just the way she liked it. They'd sit down and watch television. It was such a comforting feeling and she felt a cosy warmth embrace her body and a sense of complacency. She must remember to talk to Hugo tonight about her idea of an overseas trip. She had a delightful cruise in mind – Athens, Greek Islands, Istanbul. Yes, she'd talk to Hugo tonight. It seemed ages since they'd travelled.

Turning into the gate the car wound around the driveway and the long low house came into view, its lighted rooms revealing mysterious interiors. As if to welcome her, Hugo had switched on the verandah light outside the front door. She turned the car around ready to reverse into the garage when her attention was distracted by Minkie leaping down the steps, complaining loudly. The cat ran right up to the driver's door and stared up at Laura, mewing, her tail swishing back and forth.

Laura jumped out of the car and scooped up the agitated little creature. Minkie stared at her, her eyes huge and wild, clawing at Laura's coat.

'What's the matter darling puss? What's wrong?' Deep in her throat Minkie gave a little moan and rubbed her head beneath Laura's chin.

Entering the house Laura called out 'Hugo?'

Silence. 'Hugo!' She walked through the kitchen to the dining room. The detritus of his lunch lay on the table amongst a jumble of newspapers and files but his laptop was missing. She checked the entire house then went outside, calling into the darkening garden.

'Maybe he's just popped off into town for something' she thought. She checked the table in the entrance hall. His car keys were not there so she ran out to her car where she had left the driver's door open and pressed the remote. The garage doors hummed up. Hugo's car was gone.

Puzzled but not particularly worried Laura burrowed around in her handbag for her phone and texted *I'm home. Where r you?'* While she waited for a reply she headed for her bedroom, took off her coat, dumping her handbag on the bed and went back outside to park the car in the garage. She left the doors up for Hugo's return.

Inside she texted Hugo again, waited and then she phoned him. His phone was turned off. She felt a vague irritation and muttered 'Typical'. One of Hugo's few frustrating traits was that he was inclined to be absent minded at times and a bit careless. Feeling grumpy she returned to the dining room and started tidying up the mess on the table. A bottle of Johnnie Walker, lid off, a quarter full, stood amongst the jumble but no glass. She was pretty certain it had been a new bottle, recently replaced. Perhaps someone had called in but why no tumblers? Strange...and why were there splashes on the table and on the floor? Minkie sniffed at a puddle and reared back. She was still behaving strangely in that she was following Laura about all the time and now she was rubbing herself around her legs, looking up at her and meowing each time Laura glanced down at her. Laura did acknowledge that her behaviour was very odd – quite out of character as she was usually such a calm contented little creature.

In the kitchen she dumped Hugo's lunch cup and plate into the sink and noted that there were no used whisky glasses lying about anywhere. After screwing the top back on the Scotch and replacing it in the booze cupboard she started tidying up files. Hugo still preferred hard copies in addition to the data stored on his computer. She made a nice compact pile and then started on the newspapers.

Underneath the Sydney Morning Herald lay Hugo's phone, his set of house keys and an envelope with her name on it.

Laura's stomach took a violent lurch downwards as fear tingled in her spine and crept upwards making her throat contract and ache. Her face began to burn. She held the envelope in both hands and began to shake violently.

'Open it' she whispered – her heart pounding.

'Oh no! Please Hugo. No! You can't have...'

TREEHOUSE

Everyone agreed to take a vote. Theo had drawn the short straw and it only took a moment before they all gave him the nod. He pushed the top of the ladder with a mighty shove just as the loser's head emerged above the tree house platform. The four boys had a momentary glimpse of his startled mug before it vanished, followed by a shriek and a prolonged crashing of branches. They all sat still and listened. Silence.

They peered over the edge The forest rustled and whispered. A bird called.

They had never liked Lucas but why had they done such a cruel thing? Simple! Outsiders *must* be repelled and he just never fitted in. Too soft. Too wimpy.

With an attitude of bravado they sat down and got out the smokes. No-one spoke. They all puffed away, scanning their phones, trying to appear laconically cool.

After a while Theo said -

'D'ya think we oughta check on 'im?'

'Na – he'll be okay. He wasn't lying on the ground.' They all peered over the edge again.

'What's the time? It must be getting on for dinner.'

'Yeah' Fizz looked up at the sun and then at his phone. The shadows were lengthening. They started the long tedious process of climbing down the massive oak. The old wooden ladder lay in shattered pieces on the ground. They stood around and surveyed it.

'We're goin' t'be in trouble for that.' Paul crossed his arms.

'Yup! And that's not all.'

'Shite!' Fizz thought. King's Birthday weekend and only Day One! Bummer of a start especially when it was their first get together since the end of the Lockdown. Last thing they needed was a big blow up by the parents. He had the scary vision of his Dad losing it. But they deserved it he admitted to himself.

The group set off, soberly trailing along the shady path with none of their usual jostling and wrestling. There was certainly trouble ahead and the degree of punishment that might follow dominated their thoughts. Where was Lucas? What shape was he in? What would he say? What had he *already* said?

The imposing house came into view – its walls pale and its windows reflecting gold in the setting sun. Their parents' voices floated out of the huge room which stretched across the entire front façade of the house. Occasional bursts of laughter filtered out. Pre-dinner drinks would have started so that might be a plus. The boys skirted around the edge of the lawn amongst the trees and through the side gate into the old stable yard. There they stopped and formed a huddle.

'Whadda we going to say?' Josh scraped his foot around in the gravel, hands in his pockets. He was beginning to feel a bit sick. Fearful actually. Dad. Repercussions. They could be bloody bad when Dad lost it. Perhaps with all the others there ...

'Look' said Theo. 'It was an accident Guys. We'll just say the ladder broke. It's been there for yonks – before I was born I'll bet. It was just a piece of old crap. Really... it was, wasn't it?' He scanned the group for support.

'*Totally*. Yeah – those rungs were, like a complete hazard. Not even safe. Not steps at all.' Paul's attempt at mental reinforcement was in full production now.

Josh agreed, nodding enthusiastically. He needed a boost and confirmation from the others in the hope that, at worst, there would be some sort of group punishment to avoid Dad singling him out and raging on and embarrassing everyone.

They milled around in a close circle, scuffing up the gravel, glancing at each other for reinforcement.

'Okay' said Theo decisively. 'So we've got the story straight have we?' Fizz, Paul and Josh nodded in unison.

'C'mon – let's go then.' Theo led the way into the house.

The parents were all lolling around with drinks in their hands. The sunset was vivid through the open French doors and really gross music was playing. Utterly pathetic.

'*Well! There they all are!*' Theo's Dad, Joe Bovyer held his tankard of beer aloft as if he was about the lead a toast. The boys furtively scanned the room for Lucas and his parents. They were not in evidence.

'Had a bit of an accident did we?' Gerald Fitzallan was looking intensely at his son Jeremy whose nickname was Fizz.

'Yeah' Fizz responded quickly.

'The ladder broke.' The boys all nodded in unison.

'It was the rungs' Paul added. 'They were all rotted out.'

'Well ... the Petersons have gone to Emergency. Seems like Lucas is seriously hurt.' Gerald still had his eye firmly fixed on Fizz.

'Yeah – well – we warned him about the dicey ladder.' Fizz inspected the ceiling. 'Is he okay?' he added, as if it was a casual afterthought.

Theo's mother June chipped in.

'We'll have to wait and see, won't we?'

Uh Oh! The Truth Monitor was on the job. Avoiding her eyes Theo pretended he'd spotted something particularly interesting in the garden. Bunching up, the boys started to navigate the furniture heading for the far end of the room.

'Why didn't you bloody check on him?' Josh's father Martin raised his voice and Josh cringed. Shite! Dad was cranking up.

'Well we did Dad. We looked down when it happened and couldn't see 'im so we gathered he was okay.' Josh took a quick swig from his can of coke to try to settle his stomach. Things had seemed to be sweet where his personal involvement was concerned, up until now.

'Well he wasn't was he? Eh? Was he?' Martin was shouting now, standing up and waving his glass of scotch around. 'Why in hell didn't one of you morons call to check on him? You've all got phones for Christ's sake!'

The boys melted off, flopped into the huge leather sofas at the far end of the room and began to use the play station. Josh, following the pack, said back over his shoulder 'I dunno Dad...'

His father's face became red and it appeared that he was about to charge until Joe said

'Settle down Mart. It's okay mate. Let's wait 'til Jack and Sophie get back and we get the full story.'

The room quietened down, the parents all relaxed and chatting amongst themselves with regular replenishment of drinks and the boys trying to make themselves as unobtrusive as possible by an exaggerated concentration on the game and not too much rustling of chip packets or whooping when there was a particularly awesome win. But none of their hearts were in the game. Their twelve-year-old minds were immersed in wondering what shape Lucas might be in when he finally turned up and what he might say and ominously, what sort of punishment might be coming their way.

Tyres were scrunching on gravel followed by the slamming of car doors. The boys pretended to be immersed in their game.

The Petersons appeared – parents Jack and Sophie first and then Lucas, his left arm in a cast.

'Are you okay?' June Bovyer was fussing around. 'What happened Luc – exactly?'

The boys froze.

'I'm okay Aunty June. Honestly. I was only a short way up the ladder, just a couple of rungs so it was a short fall. His glasses were held together with a band aid and he gingerly adjusted them on his swollen nose. One of his front teeth was chipped and his left eye was almost closed with ominous swelling on his forehead.

'It was m'own fault. Had m'old sneakers on – like, no tread left. I just must've, like, y'know – slipped.' Lucas conjured up painful smile, glancing around his audience. The collection of raw scrapes and scratches on his legs and right arm were impressive.

Theo stood up and wound his way through the room.

'Hey Luc' he said, draping his arm around Lucas's shoulders causing him to wince.

'Glad you're okay mate. *Seriously* bad luck. Monster game happening between the guys dude. D'ya wanna play?'

BINS

When Angela came to live on the outskirts of the country town there were only two garbage bins provided – a red one for rubbish and a black crate for bottles. Angela's house was in a gully with a long steep drive up to the road so she would transport the black crate, which was inclined to be heavy (all those gin and tonic bottles) up to the gate in the boot of her car.

But then some of the older residents in the town started to complain about the black crates. The truck that collected them came through before 6 am in the morning and the loud noise the bottles made when they were tipped into the truck woke them up. They got a Ban the Black Bottle Bin campaign going, collecting signatures on a petition (the actual number never being revealed) and took it to Council who, true to form, crumbled to a minority and Angela now had three bins on wheels to tow up and down her driveway.

In the early years this didn't present too much of a problem but as time moved on, as did she, some weeks it was a bit of a hazard, especially when there had been rain and her driveway was slippery. Her neighbour Bessie Phillips who was in her late eighties, used a walker and obviously couldn't put her bins out anymore so Angela started to put hers out as well.

When Incident No.1 occurred it had been pouring rain and Angela timed her bin collection between downpours. She did Bessie's first. She grabbed the red bin and when she took hold of the yellow one and started to tug it was still heavy. Damn! Apparently the truck hadn't been through yet. She lifted the lid to check and to her horror the soles of two dirty sneakers like a pair of very large brown amputated ears slowly started to rise up and even more chilling, they were attached to a pair of skinny hairy legs! She involuntarily dropped the lid down but it started to rise again. The person inside was wriggling, groaning, swearing.

Angela phoned Triple Zero and the police came, tipped the bin on its side, took hold of the person's feet and pulled. The body slid out and lay on the nature strip. The rescue party were treated to a cacophony of slurred expletives. 'Drunk' said one of the cops. 'Or high' nodded the other.

The skinny little man looked to be in his fifties. He had on a pair of dirty old khaki shorts and an equally dirty black hoody and was soaking wet. The cops took him off in their cruiser to the police station and put him in the cells to sober up. He told them he was walkin' – the cops said 'more like staggerin' – along the road and when it started to teem he'd dived into the bin for shelter! He nodded sagely at the cops to confirm he had made a completely logical decision.

Incident No.2 was not so amusing. Angela had dined out on The Bin Man Incident with some comedic success but this one was a real bummer – literally. It had been raining again and she was cautiously skiddering down her drive with the empty bins when boom! Down she went. One leg shot out front ways and the other backwards followed by an interestingly athletic rollover down the bank which involved both legs coming together again in an excruciating scissor action with Angela finally coming to a halt on her back – both legs vertically in the air. The big bin (green this week) followed her, bouncing and rolling about in a very lively and aerobic way and finally coming to rest upside down, its wheels revolving slowly. 'Copycat' Angela muttered. She was known for her ironic sense of humour but this wasn't funny. The pain was unbearable as she lay there making little moans and groans. No it definitely wasn't funny as she had left her mobile in the house and it had started to rain again. 'Help!' she called out in a plaintive tentative way. But who would hear her? Only Bessie next door and she was so rickety what could she do? Well, she **could** phone an ambulance.

Angela started to scream. She tried moving but the pain in her back and other bits was agonising. Hours seemed to pass, dusk was approaching and she was so cold and then...

'Angela!' Bessie's quavery voice floated down from above. Angela turned her head upwards (ouch!) and there was Bessie and her walker silhouetted in the sunset, right up at the entrance to the driveway. A further agonising wait as poor Bessie had to make her tottery way back to her house as she only had a landline because she kept on technically mucking up her mobile or losing it and Telstra were making far too much money out of her – in her opinion.

The ambulance came.

Once Angela was back in action she had her driveway resurfaced with non-skid material. She also established a compost. But despite managing to reduce the volume of packaging she put into her yellow bin, somehow it remained as heavy as ever. Of course, she deliberately avoided counting the glassware. After all, that wee drink (or two?) before dinner did so much good to her sense of wellbeing and a fortnightly haul up the driveway (and Bessie's) did help keep her fitness at a peak.

Well... that was her story and she was sticking to it.

'Right – I understand. Well - that's a pity. Lucy won't be happy but I'll explain your rules. Thanks Jack.' Dad hung up.

I was hovering in the hallway outside the living room, fingers and arms crossed. I would have crossed my legs as well had the left one not been encumbered by a heavy white plaster. In the style of the 1950s it also had a wooden rocker attached to the bottom.

I hobbled back into my bedroom and sat on the edge of my bed in total despair. My beautiful dress hung optimistically on the wardrobe door handle.

'Forget it' I said to it. I was crying of course. Who wouldn't after such devastating news. The prospect - the totally humiliating experience that lay ahead of me - reared up in my imagination. I stared at the dress, a beautiful fifties number in blue and green tartan taffeta – ballerina skirt, stiffened petticoats and an extravagant emerald green sash. Through my tears it appeared to wobble about in watery sympathy.

Dad appeared at the door.

'Well Lu. It's bad news I'm afraid. I've just talked to Jack Bolton and...'

'I know! I heard **everything!**' I yelled, dramatically throwing myself back onto the bed, aiming for the pillows face down as I had seen in the movies. That was a flop. I just sort of rolled onto my left side anchored by the weight of the heavy plaster on my leg. I lay there and stared up at Dad and sobbed

'I can't go. I just can't. It would be too embarrassing.'

Dad regarded me impassively.

'Buck up Lu' he said. 'Get a grip. It's not the end of the world' and he ambled off.

In my small world back in the early 1950s Johnny's was the dream beginning of a teenager's social life. At fourteen years of age all the girls in my set had been hanging out for this moment for ever. Johnny's was **the** ballroom dancing school that everyone aspired to. Separated by our education in an exclusively girls' school, this was our big chance to meet boys. My school group, sitting on the lawn in the hedged sanctuary at lunchtime, had been enjoying weeks of speculation about the pending first night at Johnny's. What we were going to wear was an important point of discussion and whether our fathers would allow us to wear lipstick (Tanjee Natural of course) and nylon stockings.

For me, all this happy anticipation had been stymied by an event in the gymnasium. Resplendent in the ugly white blouses we always wore above our equally ugly pleated skirts, on this day our bottom halves sported voluminous black exercise bloomers and sandshoes. Lined up in four teams of six the brief was that we were to climb to the top of the wall bars, touch a marker at the very top, climb down like monkeys and run to the back of our line while the next girl repeated the performance. My turn. I climbed nimbly to the top, touched the marker and on my way down thought 'I'll jump.' I did and landed in a heap, my left foot shooting excruciating pains up my leg.

After school I took the bus as usual and hobbled the half mile home. Mum took a look at my foot which was swelling fast and drove me to the hospital where it was declared "a fracture" and the plaster applied.

Under normal circumstances I would have just resigned myself to six weeks of healing but all I could think of was Johnny's which was what led to Dad's phone call with the owner Jack Bolton. Dad knew him of course. Dad knew everybody. And Jack had said to Dad, once my plight had been explained, that he didn't have any time for students who didn't turn up on the first night.

'Lucy can just sit and watch' he said to Dad. 'That way she'll still be learning.'

Having left my crutches at home I hobbled into Johnny's Dance Studio on the first night and joined the other girls sitting lined up along the wall on one side of the room. I hastily covered the plaster with my copious skirt. On the other side of the hall boys were also lined up. All from private schools they were wearing their formal black suits and uncomfortable stiff white collars which they kept trying to adjust by shoving a finger down inside them and moving their necks back and forth. They all looked about twelve. They all appeared to be perspiring.

Jack Bolton walked into the centre of the room, clapped his hands and after a welcoming speech said 'Now, for starters we're going to learn The Waltz. Gentlemen! Take a partner.' The boys stood up, awkwardly shuffling their feet around. Nobody crossed the floor.

'Get moving!' shouted Mr. Bolton. 'Don't be wimps.' So, like a herd of frightened deer, boys advanced on us. They all looked terribly short.

I sat there absolutely shaking with fear. What if no-one chose me? That was the worst fear of all – to be a wallflower. But a boy was standing in front of me with his hand out.

'You from St Cuths?' It was a statement rather than a question. The St Cuthbert's Girls School uniform was a navy and blue tartan.

'No' I replied. 'I'm at EGGS.' That was Ellerton Girls' Grammar School. 'Okay' he said. 'Wanna dance?'

I looked up at him and lifted my skirt to reveal the rocker with a line of frozen toes displayed. On my working foot I wore a silver dance shoe.

'I can't dance' I whimpered. 'I broke my foot.' My potential partner looked totally brassed off and immediately started to look around for another target.

'C'mon Girl! Get up.' An immaculate man with slick blond hair had appeared. I was terrified. This, I just knew, was the notorious Mr. Stoll. His reputation preceded him, that is, strict and scary. All potential students had heard about Mr. Stoll, Mr Bolton's offsider. In our imaginations he was the equivalent of a member of the SS, World War II still featuring prominently in our history and geography curriculums.

'I can't' I stuttered, lifting my skirt higher to show him the plaster.

'For heavens' sake, then why did you come?' He was seriously irritated.

I was determined not to cry so responded defiantly 'Because Mr. Bolton told me to.'

For the next four weeks I sat meekly, leaning on the wallflower wall and observed, and then one wonderful day the plaster was removed and my dancing days began. As a reward for turning up

Mr. Bolton arranged for me to take private lessons free of charge so I could catch up. But my current losing streak appeared to continue. My personal coach was to be Mr. Stoll!

But boy!... the positive result of this absolute downer was that, despite my fear, Mr. Stoll turned me into a pretty good ballroom dancer...if I say so myself.

THAT BEAUTIFUL DAY

We have been invited to take tea at Mrs Venables'. I'm not at all inspired by the thought of even one-half hour in the company of Mrs V but my mother seems excessively excited about it and so I shall go. In a cab we often pass the Venables' house – a mansion you might say – situated on Queens Gate. It is early Georgian with a rather lovely façade. Her husband is General Anthony Venables, now returned to his previous civilian life as a KC, who inherited the house and a significant number of rural properties, both of his parents having died when he was twenty years old. He did something very brave during the War and received The Victoria Cross which, being lower than the George, was a disappointment to Mrs V – according to my mother. She says that nevertheless, they, the Venables, are waiting for him to receive a knighthood. I can hardly bear to think of Mrs V's demeanour should that happen and, if he does, no doubt she will then think it should have been higher.

Our attendance has been preceded by several days of procrastination by my mother about whether she should wear black. In the end she has settled on a full-length lilac silk tea gown, a coat of the softest grey with fur collar and a cloche hat with a substantial silk chrysanthemum plonked on the side. After a lot of argument, or should I more kindly say, negotiation, it is approved that I may wear one of my shorter gowns – the latest fashion. It is of the palest blue and has a matching loose coat with a detachable fur collar. I have shed the collar because I have chosen to wear my new broad brimmed hat and the combination of these two fashion statements, the collar and the hat, would make me appear in danger of toppling over as I am very slim, which is The Mode. I am wearing the rope of family pearls Father gave me on my eighteenth birthday.

There are quite a few other guests to tea. Some we know and those we don't are introduced to us by Mrs V who is presiding (she always presides) on a silk covered chaise longue. She is sitting at the high end, not reclining, fortunately – burdened down by copious ropes of amber and jet and crystal, which travel forward and drop over her substantial bosom like an unwieldy waterfall. She sits straight backed. Being so heavily corseted there is no possibility of her being able to recline or slouch. Her hair, no doubt dyed as it is a rather alarming colour verging on orange, appears to be lacquered and is Marcel waved. Long amber earrings complete the ensemble.

Two maids bring in the tea which is placed on a table before Mrs V who proceeds to pour out. The two gentlemen guests (both young) leap to their feet to assist with handing around. I know neither of them and suspect that it is possible that I never shall as Mrs V is in full cry on a detailed account of the death of her only son, Hubert, at Ypres. When she reaches the moment of his death I involuntarily exclaim 'Oh dear, how sad for you!' at which point she pauses, closing her eyes and then opening them again, stonily regarding me for at least ten seconds, before resuming her long dissertation. I can tell that she has related this account so many times already that it has become a script which she repeats verbatim just as an actress would do at her nightly performance.

The afternoon wears on. There is not much moving about within the vast drawing room even though there are several islands of conversationally arranged groups of chairs and chesterfields. Everyone appears to feel obliged to remain within Mrs Venables' orbit. Eventually, once the left-over cake and tea has been taken away, I pluck up the courage to rise and, affecting a casual wander across the room towards the windows, go to stand looking out as if there is something very interesting to observe. The room runs the entire depth of the house and I am looking down at the most beautiful formal garden surrounded by stone walls covered with cascading climbing roses in varieties of pink, cream and white. The centrepiece is a sandstone fountain, its water sprinkling delicately onto lily pads in a circular pond. Beyond the walls are very large English oaks and a copper beech throwing shade over that end of the wall which has a charming little folly positioned dead centre.

'Lovely, eh?'

One of the young men is standing at my shoulder. He is tall, thin, blond with a military moustache.

'Harold Tomlinson' he says, offering me his hand.

I shake it and tell him mine. We stand in silence for a moment searching for something to say and then both start to address each other at the same second. We laugh. All heads in the room turn our way.

'What are you laughing at?' shouts Mrs Venables. 'Let all of us be included in the merriment.'

'Merriment! Ridiculous woman.' I think.

However, Harold is proactive. Quick witted he replies, 'Oh...we have discovered that we have a mutual friend who is something of a maverick and were exchanging stories of his exploits.'

I am impressed that he could conjure up a credible story so glibly. I nod and smile to confirm his explanation.

'Who is it?' (This enquiry shrilly delivered.) 'Tell me as I shall surely know him.'

'Fortescue Francis' replies Harold, walking, relaxed, towards Mrs V. and therefore giving credence to his lie.

'Never heard of him' cries our hostess irritably. 'How can that be?'

She regards her guests who all react in a variety of shakes of the head, shrugs of the shoulders – only my mother looking concerned that Mrs V. might feel a failure in this instance. I feel I must rescue my Mama and so, taking a leaf from Harold's book, I conjure up a story that sadly we must go as we have another appointment over in Chelsea and, because it is almost five o'clock, the traffic will be heavy.

***

'How could you lie like that – about us having to leave?' Mother and I are standing outside on the pavement. The cab is drawing up, the driver tips his hat as he brings the horse to a halt. The butler opens the door and flushed and upset Mother gets in and just as I put my foot on the step, Harold comes running down the steps.

'May I call on you?' he asks, I nod and hand him my card. He looks pleased. As we set off, I wave to him and he gives little bow and a casual salute.

I settle back in the seat. I feel rather happy. My mother, sitting quite far from me, adjusts her position a little to face me.

'Who IS that?'

'His name is Harold Tomlinson' I reply unnecessarily as she had been introduced to him when we arrived.

'Yes...but who IS he?'

'Actually Mother, I have no idea.' I reply. And then I look at her worried face and feel sorry for her and take her hand saying, 'Don't worry. If he is a guest of Mrs Venables, he must be suitable.'

'Suitable!' I berate myself. *What a ridiculous adjective to use. It's not as if I am to marry him.'*

My mother, reassured, turns away to study The Albert Memorial, the Consort's ultimate fantasy – overloaded with sculptures and gold. She has plenty of time as we are stationary in traffic. Suddenly she gives a little start and turns again, 'I wish you had asked for *his* card.'

Harold Tomlinson's card is lying amongst the next morning's post on the silver tray on the hall table. On the back, in black ink, in a small neat hand is written – 'I shall telephone you at six o'clock this evening. H.T.'

I feel a little lurch of excitement and the delightful anticipation of the unknown.

***

My father died quite recently. He died, not in service on Flanders Field or some other awful place, but at home upon his return because of the effects of that service. He returned a completely changed man and simply died of the trauma of it all, of physical and mental exhaustion and a lingering intense fear of life.

I loved him. He was not an emotional or demonstrative man but he was a caring father to me and I know he loved me. Once I was old enough to be thoughtful to any degree I sensed that he loved me best of all of us – "us" being my mother and my older sister. But that is irrelevant. I was loved and that is all that matters.

Mother is a sweet rather ingenuous person, gentle and compliant and has never, I imagine, ever truly challenged anything of importance in her entire life. She is one of life's innocents and relied on Father entirely, and he, being the eldest boy in a large family of siblings, would never have been anything other than the dominant presence in any household and naturally controlled all the family financial arrangements.

And so, now that he has died at the relatively young age of forty-seven, my mother, totally devoid of any truly practical knowledge of anything outside domestic issues, children and a satisfactory social life, is entirely at sea. Enfolded in grief she seems unable to apply herself to anything practical at all. She is lost. It has become necessary for me to attend to the formalities of death assisted by my older sister, now at twenty-four married and expecting her first child. Together we made all the funeral arrangements with the help of her husband and that sad task being completed, we then turned our attention to the unfamiliar – money.

Our father had left a Will which, for some reason was read after the burial. I have never had any experience in the management of money. I barely thought about it as anything I needed always seemed to be available and if I should, for example, venture out on my own to shop for anything at all, I would simply say 'Please put that on the account.' and be handed the purchase without question. True, as a little child, I had every now and then had a penny placed in my tiny palm so I could hand it to the shop keeper and receive my ice cream but apart from that, money was never a factor in my thoughts.

The Will is – and this is an understatement – shocking. My father has left his entire estate to me. In retrospect I do understand that he would have been sure that my mother would have been incapable of managing any financial aspects in our lives and would want to protect us all, but nonetheless, his decision must be something of a slight to her although we have never, to this day, discussed it.

To my sister it is entirely hurtful. True, she has married well, but she, as the oldest sibling and therefore the first in the line of primogeniture, would naturally have expected to receive at least one third.

The estate itself is not in good shape. My father appears to have made some unfortunate investment decisions shortly before his death, possibly due to his fragile health and unstable state of mind. We are not poor exactly; however, the fact is that my mother and I shall have to live comparatively frugally from now on and the responsibility falls on me to ensure that our current remaining investments are carefully and conservatively managed and that any future outgoings must be limited to essentials. This is evident as I have been spending many hours in my father's study searching through papers – accounts mainly – and discovering a worrying number of unpaid bills. And as if that wasn't bad enough newspaper reports suggest that our country appears to be moving into the grip of a Depression. The only positive discovery has been that there is no mortgage on the house.

***

Harold Tomlinson has stuck to his promise. The telephone on the hall table rings in unison with the six chimes of the Sevres mantel clock in the drawing room. The maid, Dolly, answers it.

'ullo. Channing residence.'

Mother sighs. How many times has she schooled Dolly to say 'Good evening' or 'Good morning.' It appears to be a lost cause.

I take the receiver and hold it to my chest for a number of seconds. I don't want to appear as if I have been waiting. Which I have.

'Hello?'

'Hello! I hope this is not an inconvenient time.'

'Oh no... no, not at all.'

There is an awkward pause.

'I am rather hoping you are free tomorrow. The weather prediction seems good and I am wondering whether you would like to take a spin on the river? I can arrange a picnic lunch.'

'That sounds delightful. I should very much like to come.'

'Topping. Shall we say ten o'clock then?'

'Oh yes. Ten o'clock.'

'Well...good. Tomorrow then?'

'Yes – goodbye.'

'Goodbye.'

I hang up feeling completely foolish. What a pathetic exchange. I sounded like a shy schoolgirl. To be honest, I feel like one. I run upstairs before Mother can quiz me. I know she has been immobile in the drawing room, ears straining, - listening. I open my wardrobe and survey the selection of clothes. I pull out one thing then another. Too warm? Not warm enough? Too dressy? I settle on something practical and comfortable including a loose coat and a shady hat as it may be a long day to some unknown destination up or down the river and then back again. My ensemble established I return downstairs to join my mother.

***

I am in my bedroom, invisible behind the lace curtain, eyes glued to the street below. On the dot of ten a beautiful tourer pulls up and Harold, dashing in white trousers, a boater and a navy jacket with brass buttons, exits the driver's seat and disappears from sight as he approaches our front door. I note that the car's hood is down so on my way to the bedroom door I snatch a motoring veil and hover on the landing. I hear Dolly open the door and greet him. I descend the stairs slowly trying to appear relaxed. He removes his hat, looks up and smiles and says 'Good morning.' followed by an imperceptible nod of his head. Does this mean he is indicating he approves of my appearance? I am devoid of confidence about anything and guide him into the drawing room where he greets Mother and polite niceties are exchanged. Within minutes, we are leaving.

He hands me into the passenger seat, I secure my hat with the veil, tie it under my chin and we are off.

'Is it all right...the hood down? Will you be too cold? How do you feel about a drive over to Maidenhead? There is the regatta there today.'

'Oh! That sounds lovely.' I am tongue tied.

He glances at me. I worry. Is he already wondering whether he has committed to a day ahead to a companion incapable of instigating any conversation? He drives efficiently, deftly negotiating other motors and hansom cabs and eventually we are spinning through a more rural area and I start to relax, enjoying the feeling of freedom and open spaces. We comment on the various charming villages, their cottage gardens ablaze with a multitude of flowers, the pubs adorned with hanging baskets spilling over with bright blooms.

Maidenhead, bathed in sunshine is a-buzz with people, cars, horse-drawn vehicles. A band is playing. There is bunting in the town and lining the riverbank and the river is overloaded with watercraft of every description. There are long double-decker river ferries loaded to the gunnels with day trippers – men waving their hats, ladies leaning on the railings, music, a discordant combination of happy sounds. There are flat bottomed punts, the oarsmen in white shirts and trousers, deftly manoeuvring their narrow crafts with long poles. There are gondolas, the couples at the bow reclining against cushions.

Harold parks the car under a shady tree and we alight and walk a little way along the side of the river where there are gay little craft tethered. Each boat has a table in the centre sheltered by a cheerful striped canvas awning supported by four poles. Some contain parties of up to eight. We step aboard one, Harold first, turning and offering his hand to steady me. Our boatman releases the mooring rope, starts the motor and we edge out into the river.

A multitude of craft surround us. Rowers in slender skiffs, sliding silently through the water. Bulbous little clinker dinghies containing small families – occasionally a young boy straining at the oars. Unstable coracles rocking, almost stationary, containing no more than three occupants, screaming with excitement at the perilous experience. Small steamer boats with their one cheerful funnel, straight and tall and even a few brave souls sailing small yachts. It is a scene in which one just knows that the occasional accident is bound to happen.

We pass the rowing skiffs, eight young men already seated in their whites, adjusting their oars in the rowlocks, the bank thick with a variety of hats worn by the crowds of onlookers waiting for the race to begin. And then, eventually, we have rounded a bend in the river, away from all the melee and are chugging between beautiful houses, many of them timbered in the Arts and Crafts style with immaculate green lawns sweeping down to the river's edge. The Thames, that great river of so many miles and moods, is beautiful here – blue and rippling and serene. Willows, still spring green, droop down to the water hosting a variety of waterfowl busying themselves amongst the reeds.

Harold directs the boatman to find a place to tie up and once he does, a large square picnic hamper is opened and out comes a roast chicken, half a dressed ham, crisp salad, a loaf of French bread and a bottle of champagne.

'This is heavenly.' I tell Harold. 'Thank you for arranging such a beautiful day.' I open my arms and gesture towards the sky and he laughs. He knows what I am saying; that I am embracing all of it – every moment.

We eat our lunch and toast each other and feel comfortable together. He tells me about himself because I ask him. He has two sisters and an older brother. His father is a barrister, a friend of Mr Venables – they were at Oxford together. His mother paints. Harold is a junior lawyer in his father's firm. He is twenty-five and still lives at his family home in Mayfair. There is also a manor house in Norfolk and he has travelled quite often on the Continent.

I tell him about me. There isn't much to tell really but I guess, socially, he would consider me respectable. Actually, he doesn't appear to be (and it is far too early to judge) a person who has to be with socially acceptable people all the time. His sense of humour is impressive. When he talks about himself he is self-deprecating and his description of the disorganised and vivid scene we have left behind us at Maidenhead is witty but never cruel. I think *'He could be a writer.'* It seems to me he grasps atmosphere and describes people in such a vivid way, in a manner that is never demeaning or critical. It is simply that it appears that he can find so much to laugh about with a gentle affection and no malice. I feel he has a kind character. I do hope so.

***

I am thinking about that beautiful day over and over. I send him a note to thank him but already a week has passed and I have heard nothing from him. However, I am currently seriously preoccupied, trying attend to financial matters. I have an appointment with Father's accountant and financial advisor. I am very sure I can guess what he is going to advise. But we shall wait and see. Mother is accompanying me to the meeting. I would prefer she did not. I wish I had kept it a secret, however, that would have been cruel. It is just that I am nervous and suffering from a severe case of inadequacy and unease and if she were to become upset it will affect my concentration when, in a situation such as this, I must not become distracted.

So we go together. It is as I expected, we shall have to sell the house. Mother gasps, clutches her throat and begins to weep.

'No! No! This cannot happen. Not the house! No, I refuse! I have lived there all my life!'

She has. An only child, she inherited it from her parents who both, shortly after she married, died from tuberculosis within weeks of each other. It is, therefore, the only home I have ever known as I was born there. My father had been more than happy to move in, it being situated very desirably in Kensington. But we can no longer afford it – such a large residence requiring constant maintenance, the rates so high and the necessity of a number of people to staff it.

'But where shall we go?' Mother almost glares at the accountant, Mr Talbot, as if our situation is entirely his fault. I hadn't thought of that. It is possible that he has some measure of responsibility but he isn't fazed as a glare from my timid little mother is barely a glare at all. He just regards her with a compassionate expression and repeats very gently that it is vital that we sell.

***

We have sold the house quickly and at a very impressive price and have moved to a delightful and smaller house in Wimbledon. Real estate is so much cheaper on the outer fringes of London. Wimbledon is known as a garden suburb, the houses being built on comparatively large plots of land. It is leafy with quiet wide streets and its beautiful Common so conveniently nearby – so pleasant for taking long walks and cycling.

But Mother is bereft. Nobody, least of all Mrs Venables, invites her any more to any function at all. The mantlepiece in the drawing room no longer displays a reliable crowd of embossed invitations. She has been demoted by her unsuitable geographic location. She would have to take the train to reach them – her once-upon-a-time friends! And it is far too far for them to think of visiting her. No! She is completely socially shunned.

I don't mind. I like taking walks and we are not far from the river and Hampton Court – so lovely for a leisurely day out. And we have purchased a car which I drive. Now, as the Twenties begins, a number of women have learnt to drive cars. Mother and I are now mobile and entirely independent.

When we moved, Dolly left us to go and work in a factory. 'Much higher wages' she informed us in a slightly accusatory tone and besides, on her days off she prefers the bright lights.

Dear Mrs Kerr, the cook, is a widow and was happy to come with us. She likes a bit of peace and quiet and the comfort that our home provides as she lives in. And we now have a new maid, Eunice, who lives out, still with her parents, and comes to us daily from Putney on the bus. Our gardener, Mr Price, is a gem. We inherited him from the previous owners who were, according to Mr Price, very horticulturally knowledgeable. The house has a beautiful garden.

I am busy. I have joined the Women's Suffrage. We are at last appearing to be making good progress with The Cause. I have also joined a group of women who meet to discuss literature, some of whom are published authors. One of these women, Clarice, and I have become friends. She drives as well so we have formed a small motoring club, women only, and drive out, in convoy, to the countryside on weekends.

I have never heard from Harold and I hear no news of him as I too must now be considered persona non grata geographically, although I do travel into London on the train to attend The Suffrage meetings.

I am now twenty-six and have joined a generation of young single women who are my age – or younger or older. The War demolished so many young women's expectations and hopes.

I never thought to ask Harold why he hadn't served...on that beautiful day.

TYPHOON

I think I'll start a journal. I'm going to be twelve next week and there'll be loads of interesting stuff happening from now on I expect. But first, perhaps I should write down the most scary thing that has happened to me – so far...

My name is Christo and I'm twelve years old and I reckon that so far my life has been pretty interesting. I live in Australia but I was born in Fiji which is in the South Pacific Ocean. My Dad is Australian so he made me an Australian citizen immediately. He had a job that meant we had to move around quite a lot to different countries. I didn't mind it too much although it was always difficult when I had to leave my friends and feel lonely in a new school in another country and the saddest thing was when we had to give our dog Jumper away to some friends when we were leaving The Philippines. We went back to see him a few years later and he remembered us and the best thing about that visit was to see how happy he was.

There are some interesting things I can remember when I was young like the island we used to go to on weekends while we were still living in Fiji. The most amazing thing that happened there was that one day I was sitting on a mound of sand on the beach and suddenly hundreds of baby turtles started to hatch and pop up out of the sand all around me and scurry towards the water. They were a lovely green colour and so tiny. All the kids tried to help them reach the sea.

I remember our house in Fiji which had a big garden and lots of trees. It was down next to the sugar cane fields. I started to do carpentry. I had a hammer and some big nails and pieces of board and I used to nail them to the trees and paint signs on them, mainly to prevent my sister from invading my space when her irritating girlfriends came over to play.

But the biggest thing I remember about Fiji were the hurricanes. We lived beside the airport and a loud siren would go off and trucks would come around to all the houses and the smiling Fijian men riding on the back would leap off and drag out the wooden pallets stored under our house and attach them to our windows. This was to prevent stuff breaking our windows when it was flying about in the storm. Mum would scoot around the house turning off the electricity and gas and closing up all the windows and doors. The hurricanes were pretty scary I must say and left a big mess after they had finished. Trees would blow down and the Fijians' bures (that was the name of their houses) would lose their roofs and one time our revolving clothesline was bent in half.

***

While I was still young we went to live in Manila which is the capital city of The Philippines. It was so different. Manila was huge with millions of people living there. Lots of them were poor and lived in squatters huts which they built themselves from all kinds of stuff they found lying around. It was strange though because they all seemed to have a television aerial and there were masses of electric wires tangled up all over the place. I never understood that. It looked like black spaghetti.

When we arrived in Manila we lived in an awesome hotel for a few weeks. We were on the 15th floor and one night there was an earthquake and the building swayed a bit and the beds my sister and I were sleeping in moved away from the wall. The swimming pool was down on the 5th floor and we looked out the window and saw the water swishing backwards and forwards and spilling over the side of the building down onto the street. It was a huge waterfall.

Besides that scary experience it was fun living in the hotel because we could swim in the pool every day and Ben who looked after our rooms was really cool. He had a trolley with lots of clean towels on it and two humungous bags hanging off for the dirty washing. He would leave one bag empty for me to stand in and I'd ride along with him to each room. Keep in mind I was a lot smaller then. He'd give me Cokes and chocolates that were left in the rooms after the guests had gone.

The house we moved into was in a huge village. It had a massive security wall that ran all the way around it. There was one big gate with guards to let us in. They carried guns. Our house also had a very high wall with glass spikes along the top and when you were inside you couldn't see anything outside except the tops of trees.

School was really weird. We went there at 7 o'clock in the morning and came home at 1.30 in the afternoon. This was because it was so hot. We had so much homework it really sucked. Sometimes we wouldn't go to school at all because there was a teachers' strike or a bomb scare or floods. One morning we arrived at school and were told that there was a typhoon coming. Typhoons are the same as hurricanes. Of course my sister and I thought it was ace that we were going to have another day off but when we got home Mum was pretty fed up. She started to rave on about all the days of school we were missing. My sister and I tried not to listen to her and went into the TV room to watch cartoons.

Dad rang up from his office and told Mum that there definitely was a typhoon coming and that she should start getting the house ready. In Manila there were no people coming around on trucks to put shutters up on our windows. Mum had staff called maids to help around the house so we all got busy turning off electricity and gas, closing up windows and running around the garden putting anything inside that might blow around when the typhoon came.

First of all it started to rain like mad and the wind quickly got wild. It was roaring so loudly we had to shout at each other and eventually we couldn't see anything outside. It was entirely white and we could only see spooky shapes flying past like TV aerials, bits of timber and trees. Water was coming in through the louvre windows which are sort of like glass plantation shutters. Soon all the floors were covered in water and we were slopping around in it up to our ankles. The typhoon was crashing onto the front of our house so Mum ran to the back and opened a window just a crack. She had been taught to do this in Fiji at Hurricane Drill because, apparently, it stopped pressure building up inside the house which could cause the roof to blow off. We were all extremely scared. We had never known a hurricane as bad as this. The noise was so terrible and so much water was pouring inside.

Suddenly the storm stopped and it became very still and quiet. It wasn't even raining but we still couldn't see outside. It was completely white. Mum yelled 'It's the eye! We're in the eye of the typhoon!' She ran down to the back of the house to close the window. Then there was a massive explosion. My sister and the maids were all screaming and crying they were so frightened. So was I even though I tried not to. The typhoon suddenly came back again and slammed onto the back of our house. Mum came shooting back into the living room and the six of us all huddled together against the wall away from the windows. At last the typhoon moved away (whew!) and there was just pouring rain. The lady next door turned up. The explosion was the noise when her roof blew off. We looked out the window and part of it had landed on the side of our roof and was covering our driveway. She should have got typhoon advice from Mum.

Dad's office was down on the sea front next to the harbour and all the windows blew out. He told us big cargo ships ended up against the sea wall opposite his building and the city was in total destruction. He said it was the worst typhoon that had ever hit Manila. It was called 'Yoling'. Days later when the roads were clear we went to see all the disaster.

I woke up really early the morning after the typhoon and it was sunny with no wind at all. I went outside to look at the damage and there was a big piece of roof lying in our driveway with nails and pieces of wood and stuff all scattered around. I ran inside and woke up Dad and told him it was one of the happiest days in my life because I had a whole roof for my carpentry. He reckoned I was the only happy person in Manila that day.

We went to live in other countries but Australia rocks. It is my forever home.

IT'S ONLY THE PACKAGING

When was it that I started to feel old? Well – so far – never. Not really. Y'know – not in the mind. There are a few achy bits now and then I admit. But generally it is my plan to remain a box of birds.

Are all news reporters under thirty years old? I ask this because it seems they regularly refer to anyone over fifty as elderly. For example, if, at sixty-five, I had been hit by a bus and actually achieved a mention in *The News*, the report would say, 'Elderly woman survives road accident.' Elderly! For heaven's sake! At sixty-five I was running a business, climbing ladders, in my prime! Twenty years later I am still running that business. It's forty-five years old, more than half my age. But I no longer do ladders. That's Wisdom – a major positive. Wisdom keeps on growing every day we are alive.

At sixty I began to think about that word never to be spoken – 'aging.' The Parents were complaining about it. 'Not me. It'll never happen to me' I told myself, so as a form of assurance I made The List. I've always been a compulsive list maker. According to my mother, in 1960 when I was twenty-one and planning my wedding which, she told me, I organised entirely on my own although Mum and Dad paid, something really critical on The List went out of plum which resulted in a major drama – well – in my mind apparently. Upon reflection, a bit of drama has always added spice to my life. My prospective husband, a relaxed sort of bloke at thirty-two years' old and therefore having already achieved 32% of his Wisdom, remarked to my mother 'Well, bang goes that list'.

So at sixty-five I added a really important list to my lifetime of lists and I gave it a title.

"OLD DUCKDOM"

I added a stern reminder. "To be avoided at all costs."

The List contained a resolute itemisation of plans with the addition of a few tips.

1. <u>Same Old Stories</u>

    Try very hard to remember which reminiscence you've told to whom.

2. <u>Money</u>

    Don't be a meanie. Some oldies are just plain stingy.

3. <u>Granny in the Corner</u>

    Something to say? Don't bother. Nobody younger will be interested.

4. <u>Wear whatever you like</u>

    Appropriately trendy is okay and "Lippy" is allowed.

5. <u>Name all those people in the faded photographs</u>

    Unlikely to be appreciated or incite interest but never mind.

6. <u>Tidy up and throw out</u>

    Sort and discard in consideration to whoever may have to tidy up after you.

7. <u>Write it Down</u>

    Your life is yours. It's exclusive. There is no other exactly like it and it is worth everything to you, so

record it – not only for your own fulfillment but also
to prove that you actually existed at all!

Well – that was The List. So far I have passed three and failed four. I must strive to do better as suddenly time seems to be on overdrive.

What is that? The speed of time which appears to increase its forward movement the older we get? Well… I put it down to keeping busy. There is too much to do in a day. Forget the housework or creating trendy meals. I keep company with Wisdom. At 84% I'm getting towards top marks but I very much doubt I want to achieve 100%. It sounds far too rickety.

AND… that leads to another word, never to be spoken. "Death".

Mark Twain said,

'I do not fear death. I had been dead for billions and billions of years before I was born and had not suffered the slightest inconvenience from it.'

How sensible that is. I'm glad I've dealt with that subject in such a reassuring manner. You see! That's Wisdom for you.

Lately I've become aware that I don't see myself as others see me. Does that concern me? Well yes – I am appalled to realise it does as recently I experienced the following encounter. Here I am, capably hauling groceries into the boot of my car and a voice says 'Can I help you with that?' and I turn to see a stranger, a woman who is at least seventy, who is smiling at me in what I perceive to be a sympathetic way. I snap 'No thanks!' and then, sitting behind the wheel preparing to drive off I feel absolutely dreadful. How could I have been so horrible to such a kind person? What was that? Pride or worse, Vanity rearing its head? How can it be that outside

I must look so terribly old when inside I feel just as sparky as I have throughout all of my life? The same zest for life. The same sense of humour, happiness at times – sadness. The same bouts of irritation or worse, anger? The same love and appreciation of family, friends and all things aesthetic?

I turn my head and there is Wisdom, regarding me through the driver's window with an expression of such understanding and saying, 'That is correct. The essence of you has remained the same. Inside you are no different. It's definitely the packaging.

***

PEACE IN PRAGUE

To Prague I went. I talked to a girl. When the wall came down this girl had just finished her education. As I talked with the girl she described the Soviet occupation and the terrifying restrictions to every citizen's way of life.

As, nearly three decades later, I reflect on this encounter I can't help but relate, to some lesser degree, to what we have been experiencing in these recent times when an enemy was created in the form of a virus and our basic freedoms taken from us in so many ways.

This girl told me how much her people had longed to be free. She told me how all citizens in the now optimistic Czech Republic – Czechia – were striving to learn English. She was ecstatic that international tourists were beginning to filter back into her beloved Prague. They were so welcome she said. Freedom was theirs at last and the fearful life, all she had ever known since birth, had dissolved.

***

To Prague I went. To all the major concert halls and theatres.

At the Estates Theatre a Dickensian old man took me on a tour. He was very thin and frail. He played excerpts from Mozart on an ancient clavichord. His energy and enthusiasm and devotion to his job and The Master made me want to cry. I stood where Mozart had stood to conduct the first performance of Don Giovanni. That evening I returned and sat in a box on a little blue velvet chair and watched the performance.

***

To Prague I went and visited the Mozart Cafe. I ordered extravagant cake. I sat at a table in a window directly opposite the face of Orloj, the 15th century astronomical clock. The face of the clock was there, looking back at me into the tearoom. I leaned out of the window and looked down into The Square. Below me great crowds of people gathered waiting for the hour. Milling, swirling, waving – a momentarily united mass of happy anticipation, of movement and colour and sound.

The Clock began its performance. The revolving mediaeval men performed their routine of 600 years. The skeletons on either side of the clock face gestured downwards and mocked the audience. 'Here be the future.'

***

To Prague I went. I walked beside the river to The Rudolfinum and sat before the orchestra; beneath the ornate ceiling; amongst an audience speaking every language, united in their love of music. The atmosphere, the music - it enveloped me. The swaying bodies of the musicians. Their gorgeous instruments. United. Co-operating. Working as one. Creating such stirrings of the heart, such moving emotions of peace, sublime happiness, elation, sadness. That beautiful music.

Ah Yes! An idealistic longing, a wistfulness, that this world, this glorious revolving sphere and every being clinging to it could thus be so united.

To Prague I went.

About the Author

Born in New Zealand in 1938, Lorraine James has lived an expatriate life across the UK and Southeast Asia, including Hong Kong and the Philippines. After moving to Australia she lived in Sydney for nearly twenty years, founding her giftware company Kate Finn in 1978 and continuing to travel widely over the next four decades. She moved to live in the Southern Highlands in 1995, continuing, with her designer daughter, to distribute luxury nursery and children's products throughout Australia and New Zealand. Since semi-retirement in 2019, Lorraine has devoted herself to writing short fiction as a member of the Fellowship of Australian Writers, culminating in her first collection, *Flights of the Mind*.

www.ingramcontent.com/pod-product-compliance
Lightning Source LLC
Chambersburg PA
CBHW031231210726
48287CB00003B/734